NED OAKS

DECEPTION CREEK

Complete and Unabridged

LINFORD
Leicester

First published in Great Britain in 2016 by
Robert Hale
An imprint of The Crowood Press
Wiltshire

First Linford Edition
published 2018
by arrangement with
The Crowood Press
Wiltshire

*A catalogue record for this book is available
from the British Library.*

ISBN 978–1–4448–3824–4

Published by
F. A. Thorpe (Publishing)
Anstey, Leicestershire

Set by Words & Graphics Ltd.
Anstey, Leicestershire
Printed and bound in Great Britain by
T. J. International Ltd., Padstow, Cornwall

This book is printed on acid-free paper

DECEPTION CREEK

A masked predator is stalking the town of Oakridge. Known as the Phantom, he strikes at night, attacking sleeping couples in their beds, raping and murdering with impunity. Despite the best efforts of the local deputy, he manages to elude capture, and finally former marshal Ed Burton is brought in to assist the investigation. Working with Deputy Sheriff Maynard Blayloch, he becomes obsessed with his quarry, and soon they close in on a suspect. But nothing is what it seems, and suddenly Burton finds himself the target of the Phantom . . .

1

The man in the burlap mask stood silently in the darkness for a couple of minutes, watching the sleeping couple in their bed. He had slipped into the house without waking either of them.

There was a lantern turned down low on a table near the bedroom door. In the dim light he could see the shape of a man lying on his side on the far side of the bed. A woman lay beside him, her long coppery hair spread out on her pillow.

They were sleeping deeply. The man in the mask's heart was beating so rapidly that he worried they would hear it and wake up. He smirked slightly. It was a stupid thought. All of his senses were sharply attuned in preparation for what he was about to do.

He picked up the lantern in his left hand and stepped toward the end of the bed. In his right hand he clutched a Colt .44 pistol. Suddenly he turned up the lantern to its full brightness, spilling light across the bedroom. Neither the man nor the woman awakened. Irritated, the masked stranger smashed the butt of his pistol into the sleeping man's ankle, waking him immediately.

The man yelled in pain, startling his wife awake. She screamed when she saw the intruder with the pistol.

'Shut up!' hissed the man in the mask. He thrust the gun forward, speaking through clenched teeth. Two holes had been cut out of the mask, revealing his pale blue eyes. Those eyes moved rapidly back and forth between the man and the woman in the bed, scanning for any signs of resistance.

'Who the hell are you?' yelled the man in the bed.

'I said shut up!' snapped the stranger.

He put the lantern back on the table and pulled a handful of pre-cut lengths of rope from his pocket. He tossed these on to the bed, then pointed the barrel of the gun at the woman, who by this time had tears streaking down her cheeks. She was struggling to sob quietly — she didn't want to provoke him by making any more noise.

'Tie him up!' he commanded. His voice had a shrill quality to it, almost as if he were trying to disguise it. He seemed nearly as scared as the woman.

She hesitated momentarily, her mind struggling to process the unfolding situation.

'Do you want to die?' the man in the mask screamed. He brought the gun down hard on her shin.

'N-n-no,' she said, taking the ropes in her hand. She turned to her husband, whose gaze was locked on the figure at the end of the bed. He turned and looked at the ropes. He seemed dumb with fear and confusion.

'Do it!' the stranger yelled.

He fired a bullet into the wall a few inches above her head. She yelped. Her husband put his hands behind his back and she tied his wrists.

'Tighter!' the man barked.

She tightened the knot as he watched.

'Now his ankles!'

She tied her husband's ankles, making sure to pull the knot extra tight.

'Turn around.'

She did as she was ordered, putting her hands behind her back. He tied her quickly and expertly. He pulled the knots extremely tight, to the point where she winced. The knot he used was elaborate and unusual, but guaranteed not to come undone. He ignored her pain. When he finished tying her up to his satisfaction, he retied the knots on her husband, then dragged him off the edge of the bed on to the floor. He checked the knots again to make sure the man was completely immobilized before rising and abruptly leaving the room without another word.

'Oh, God, Pete,' the woman said quietly. Her name was Margaret Dexter. 'What's he going to do?'

'I don't know,' Pete Dexter said,

despair in his voice.

They heard footsteps coming toward them from down the hallway. The woman whimpered softly, fear a powerful force within her. She felt an overwhelming sense of helplessness. Only two or three minutes had elapsed since the man had awakened them, but it felt like a lifetime.

The man in the mask came back into the room. In his hands he carried a small stack of plates and two porcelain cups. He walked to Pete Dexter and placed the dishes in two stacks on the prone man's back.

'You make any move and I'll hear these dishes rattle,' he said. 'I hear these dishes rattle and you die.' He jerked a thumb toward Margaret Dexter. 'And she dies, too.' He leaned forward and pressed the end of his gun barrel against the man's temple. 'I will kill you.'

His voice was harsh and grating, and Pete Dexter had no doubt that he meant what he said.

5

'I won't move.'

The man rose and pulled Margaret Dexter to her feet. He pushed her toward the hallway, and she had to hop ahead of him with her ankles bound. Pete heard them make their way to the living room, heard his wife's muffled sobs, heard the man's voice dispensing commands. He knew what was taking place in that room.

Sweat poured down his forehead; his wrists and ankles had moved past the stage of throbbing pain toward numbness. He wondered whether the man in the mask would kill them, and concluded that he would. There was a palpable rage within the attacker, as if the Dexters themselves had violated him. Pete searched his mind but was unable to place the stranger. The mask and the strangely altered voice had succeeded in obscuring his identity, if indeed he was someone familiar to the Dexters.

Pete heard fast approaching steps and suddenly the man in the mask was standing over him, his breathing heavy. His paranoid hands felt the knots, and then he was gone, once more striding rapidly to the living room.

Margaret Dexter's quiet pleas began again.

2

Ed Burton sat atop his horse, looking toward the mountains that ringed his new home. They were densely covered by tall, majestic fir trees, over which lay a thick, almost impenetrable layer of mist. The cold air had a bite to it, and he pulled up the collar of his sheepskin around his dark beard. There was moisture on the lenses of his glasses.

He was on a trail not far from Oakridge, in the southern end of the Willamette Valley. After breakfast that morning, he had decided to ride into town and pick up some items at the mercantile. He had stopped to fasten the top two buttons on his coat, then became distracted by the forbidding beauty of the nearby mountains. He had been raised in this area but had spent several years as a town marshal on the other side of Oregon. His return to the place where he had spent his childhood sometimes triggered uncharacteristic moods of nostalgia, as it did now. He thought about how many times he had gazed upon those hills when he was still just a kid.

So many years later, they still had the power to move him.

Burton was contemplating the misty peaks when he heard the rider coming toward him on the trail. He pulled the reins on his horse and turned around. He recognized the approaching horseman as Maynard Blayloch, the deputy sheriff in Oakridge. He smiled and nodded at Blayloch as the lawman pulled up near him.

'Morning, Maynard,' he said genially.

'Good morning, Mr Burton,' said the deputy, with more than a touch of deference.

Blayloch was a clean-shaven man of average build, in his early thirties. He was well aware of Burton's background in police work. Some of Burton's cases had been covered in the newspapers, before he resigned his position in eastern Oregon and returned to Oakridge. The two men had even discussed a few of them. They were on friendly terms.

There was an awkward silence.

'What brings you out this way?' asked Burton.

'Well, we got a problem,' said Blayloch. 'I was wondering if you could spare a little time and advise me on something. I didn't want to bother you, but the sheriff insisted I ask.' He shifted in the saddle. 'You ever remember hearing about the Phantom?'

Burton frowned. 'I do, yes. That was quite a few years ago, though, wasn't it?'

'Yep, it was. Five years since the last time he struck — until last night.'

'I see,' said Burton thoughtfully. The horrors of his last case as town marshal had led to his resignation and subsequent return to the land of his youth. He was wary of any further involvement in police work, as Maynard Blayloch knew. But his interest was piqued.

'He attacked Pete and Margaret Dexter at their cabin sometime after midnight,' Blayloch explained. 'I'm heading over there to talk with them. I'd be much obliged if you would join me.'

'I'd be glad to,' said Burton.

* * *

Burton and Blayloch rode into the Dexters' yard about an hour later. The door to the cabin was open. They hitched their horses to the post by the front porch, climbed the steps, and entered the house, removing their hats as they did so.

Margaret Dexter sat on the couch in the living room. She was wrapped in a blanket. Pete Dexter stood by the entrance to the hallway. Both seemed slightly stunned, as if they had experienced something they couldn't quite accept or understand.

'Morning, Margaret,' said Blayloch. He nodded at her husband. 'Pete.' He gestured toward Ed Burton. 'This is Mr

Ed Burton. He used to be a town marshal over in — '

Burton cleared his throat. 'We've met before, Maynard.'

'Oh, sorry,' said Blayloch, his face flushing. 'Well, as I was saying, Pete, Mr Burton has lots more experience with this sort of thing than I do. I thought he might be able to help.'

Pete Dexter merely nodded.

'Can you tell us what happened?' asked Burton.

'It must've been after two in the morning,' Dexter began. 'We was asleep. Man in a mask woke us up. He had a gun on us both.' He paused, and Burton and Blayloch waited patiently while he gathered his thoughts. 'He had Margaret tie me up, and then he tied her. He tied us real tight.' Dexter raised his wrists and displayed them for the two men. They bore angry-looking purple welts, and his hands were still discolored from the lack of circulation. 'Margaret's hands and feet are the same.'

Burton glanced quickly toward her,

but she had covered her entire body with the blanket, which was pulled all the way up to her neck.

Maynard Blayloch reluctantly prodded Pete Dexter for more details.

'What happened then, Pete?'

'He put me on the floor. Got some dishes and put them on my back. Told me he'd kill us both if he heard them dishes rattle.'

Burton and Blayloch exchanged glances. Burton remembered that the rapist known as the Phantom had often used this technique in his attacks from years ago.

Dexter continued: 'Then he took Margaret and . . . had his way with her.' The profound trauma of the previous night was etched across his face. He looked up quickly when he heard Ed Burton's voice.

'Do you think you knew this feller?' Burton asked.

Dexter shook his head. 'No. At least, not as I could tell. He had that mask on and his voice sounded odd. Only thing

13

we could make out was his eyes. Real blue, they were.'

'How'd he get in?'

'Pried open a window in the kitchen. He must have been real quiet.'

'Well, he's done this before,' observed Burton. 'You ever heard of the Phantom?'

Margaret Dexter raised her head, a startled expression crossing her face.

'You think this was him?' she asked anxiously.

Maynard Blayloch, as the official law enforcement officer at the scene, spoke up. 'Ma'am, it sounds an awful lot like him. We can't say for sure, but it's more than likely.'

'He said he'd been watching us,' the woman said. 'That he'd been planning on doing this for a long time.'

Pete Dexter suddenly hit the log wall hard with his fist. He turned and walked down the hallway.

'Pete . . . ' his wife murmured, then covered her face with her hands. She cried quietly.

'Ma'am, I hate to ask you more questions at a time like this, but I've only got a couple more. I'd like to get out of here and let you and Pete be alone.'

She nodded, her face still covered by her hands. She breathed deeply, and after a moment she removed her hands. She had stopped crying.

'Please ask your questions, Mr Blayloch,' she said.

'Thanks, Mrs Dexter. Now, when did he leave?'

'A couple hours after he got here. He took his time. He even ate some food at the table while we were tied up. Then I heard the back door open and after a while I knew he was gone. It took me a long time, but I finally got the bindings loose on my wrists. After I got free, I untied Pete. He couldn't even feel his hands or feet anymore.'

'I guess it was right after that that Pete rode over to my place,' suggested Blayloch. He lived not far from the Dexters, on a forty-acre spread.

'Yes, it was.'

'My last question, ma'am,' said Blayloch delicately. 'Did he say anything else that you think might be useful for us in apprehending him?'

Margaret took a moment to consider his question. Finally, she shrugged.

'I don't think so, Mr Blayloch. He promised to kill us over and over again. He kept ranting. Eventually I realized he just wanted us to obey him, so I tried to do everything he asked.' She blushed. 'He was so angry I was sure we were going to die. I don't know how we survived.' Her eyes met Burton's. 'I'm sure he'll kill someone, Mr Burton. Sooner or later, that's what he'll do. Maybe he didn't have the guts to do it last night, but it will happen. I can just feel it.' She fell silent, gazing absently at the floor.

Burton realized that they were standing in the room where she had been violated. He felt a powerful urge to leave.

'Well, Maynard,' he said. 'Probably best we be headin' out.'

'What? Oh, yes. Absolutely.' Blayloch pushed a lock of hair out of his eyes and began backing toward the door. 'Mrs Dexter, we thank you so much for your assistance. I'll be getting to work on finding this sidewinder right away.'

She smiled faintly in acknowledgement of Blayloch's words. She was through talking for the moment. Burton said nothing. He followed Blayloch out of the door and closed it behind them. They untied their horses and began to walk across the yard, holding the animals by the reins.

'What do you make of it, Mr Burton?' asked Blayloch.

Burton was pensive. 'It's got to be him,' he said. 'The Phantom.'

'I think so, too.'

'Wonder why he was out of action for so many years.'

'Could've been in jail.'

'Quite possibly.'

'Or maybe he moved somewhere, but now he's moved back.'

They stopped at the edge of the yard

and mounted their horses, then started up the trail through the forest. Burton observed the overcast sky and knew there would soon be rain.

'How many times did the Phantom attack?' he asked.

'Four times that we know of,' said Blayloch. 'I have always wondered if there were other attacks that no one ever told us about. Some people might have a real hard time telling the law about something like this.'

'That wouldn't surprise me,' Burton agreed. He liked the way Blayloch thought. Here was a man who took his job seriously, just as Burton always had.

'He did the same thing back then that he did with Pete and Margaret Dexter,' Blayloch said. 'Breaking into people's homes in the dead of night. He was always able to get in without being heard. He'd wake them up, hold a gun on them to make them do as they were told, and then tie them up.'

'He did his little trick with the dishes, too.'

'Yes. He did that in every case that I know of.'

They emerged from the trees into a large forest pasture, hundreds of acres wide. They rode across the moist grass, watching the mist drift down from the hills into the valleys.

'You could see how bad it was for Margaret,' said Blayloch. 'Pete's going to torture himself. All the men who've encountered the Phantom have been changed permanently. They all think there was something more they could have done, or that their wives only think of them as half a man now.'

Burton adjusted his spectacles. 'Looking down the barrel of a gun changes the way a man looks at life,' he noted. He spoke from experience. 'It makes a man understand himself in a way he didn't before. Sometimes that's a painful understanding.'

'I would imagine so,' said Blayloch. He had never so much as been shot at in his six years of work as a deputy sheriff.

'But you can't forget that if Pete Dexter had resisted, had shown any sign of fighting back against this . . . Phantom — well, I have no doubt that they'd both be dead right now.'

'You think so?'

'I do,' Burton said. 'And I think Pete Dexter knows that, too.' There was pity in his voice. 'The man had no other choice if he wanted to stay alive, and help his wife stay alive, too.'

★ ★ ★

It was mid-afternoon when Ed Burton rode into the small barn behind his house. He unsaddled his horse and brushed it, then forked some fresh hay into its stall and gave it some oats.

When he entered the house, Annie Burton was sitting on the couch by the window in the living room. She was knitting. On the other end of the couch, three kittens lay snuggled up to their mother, a large tortoise-shell cat that the Burtons had inherited along with the house and property after the death of Annie's father the year before.

Burton had never thought of himself as a man who could like a cat, but he had rapidly changed his mind and felt so much affection for the animal that he was sometimes inwardly embarrassed. The big tortie hadn't had a name when they moved in, so Burton's wife had taken to calling her Edith.

'Where you been?' asked Annie Burton as her husband removed his boots.

'I been helping ol' Maynard with something.'

She arched an eyebrow. 'Is that right?'

He removed his hat and peeled off his coat.

'Yes, that's right,' he said. He was slightly irritated by her curiosity, particularly since he had renounced any involvement with law enforcement after their return to Oakridge.

'What kind of help did Maynard need?' she enquired.

Burton walked over and petted Edith and her kittens.

'You remember a rapist they called 'the Phantom'?' he asked.

'From around here?'

Burton nodded. 'Attacked at least four couples in their cabins in the middle of the night. Raped the wives while the husbands were tied up, either watching or listening.'

All the humor had left Annie Burton's face. 'I don't think I remember this Phantom,' she said. 'Was there anything in the papers about it?'

'Some, yes. I remember talking about it with your pa and some of the locals when we came and visited a few years back.'

'So they never caught him?'

'He stopped. They never got the chance to catch him.'

'What's this got to do with you and Maynard Blayloch?' she asked.

Burton sat down in a chair across the room from his wife. Sunlight streamed in through the window over her head.

'Well, the Phantom struck again last night. For the first time in five years.'

Annie Burton looked alarmed. And justifiably so, thought her husband.

'Who was it?' she asked.

'Pete and Margaret Dexter,' said Burton. His wife took in a sharp breath. She knew and liked both of the Dexters, and had grown up in the Oakridge area with them before they were married.

'What did he do?' she asked.

'He snuck into their cabin in the middle of the night. Held them hostage with a pistol and raped Margaret.'

'Lord above,' said Annie Burton, her face drawn. 'Poor Margaret.'

'Pete, too. He's in bad shape. Not as bad as she is, but still . . . pretty bad.'

'Of course. Do you think there's anything I can do for them?' She put her knitting down in her lap, eager to help the Dexters.

Ed Burton held up a hand. 'Slow down, there. I don't think they want to see anyone today, except maybe their kin. Anyway, Maynard told them we'd keep it real discreet.'

She sat back, then picked up her needles again. Burton thought her mind was no longer on her work.

'I understand,' she said.

He stared out of the window toward the treetops beyond. She continued knitting. Neither spoke for a while.

'You should help Maynard,' she said suddenly. 'You've handled these kinds of things before. He could use that experience. I don't think you should just stand by and — '

'I'm not just going to stand by and leave it all to Maynard,' he countered. 'I know I said I was done as a lawman, but this is different. This Phantom is going to kill someone if he's not stopped. He swore he would kill the Dexters. They're not sure why he didn't.'

'Did Pete or Margaret get a look at him?'

Burton shook his head. 'He wears a mask. Only thing they remember is that he has blue eyes. But hell, Pete Dexter and Maynard both have blue eyes, too.'

Annie Burton knew her husband would be automatically noting the eye color of every man he met until the Phantom had been identified. It was part of his compulsive approach to his work.

'So what are you going to do next?' she pressed. 'Doesn't seem like you can do much more right now than wait for him to do it again.'

'Even if he does, it'll be damn near impossible for us to catch him as things stand. Unless he slips up and some husband is able to get his hands on a gun. That would put an end to things right quick.'

He idly watched the rapid movement of his wife's needles as she knitted, his mind considering the attack on the Dexters. He had a few questions he wanted to discuss with Maynard Blayloch.

3

Lucy Bickham's eyes were open, although she didn't know why.

It was pitch black in the small farmhouse, and she had been asleep for at least a few hours. She rolled over on to her back and looked beside her. Her husband, Everett, was sleeping soundly. He snored occasionally in the darkness as his wife watched him for a few moments. She laid her head back on the pillow and closed her eyes.

Then she heard it again, and realized what had awakened her.

It was the sound of glass breaking.

She sat up, turning her ear toward the sound, which had come from somewhere down the short hallway leading from her bedroom to the kitchen and living room. She heard more sounds now — quiet, cautious sounds of someone moving around in the darkness.

She reached out and shook her sleeping husband's shoulder.

'Ev,' she said quietly. She shook him a little harder and leaned close to his ear. 'Ev!' she said again, this time with more urgency.

He opened his eyes and looked at her.

'What's wrong?' he asked groggily.

'I heard something down the hall. I think someone's in the house.'

Ev Bickham was fully awake now. He reached toward the small table beside the bed and removed his pistol from the top drawer. He stood up stealthily, moving toward the hallway, pistol in hand. He stopped there to listen.

He heard nothing as he stood there listening, but he knew his wife wasn't the kind of woman who imagined noises in the night. He knew she had heard something.

He turned and crept quietly down the hallway, past his daughter's room. Her door was slightly ajar and he could see her sleeping peacefully in her bed.

The noise her mother had heard hadn't awakened her. He continued past her doorway toward the living room and stopped for a moment before looking in. Hearing nothing, he stepped into the room, his pistol extended in his hand.

He was, for a few seconds, too shocked by what he saw to respond.

A man stood with his back to Bickham. He was pulling a mask over his head. He wore a thick flannel shirt but no pants.

'Who the hell are you?' Bickham asked loudly.

The Phantom turned. Bickham could see the man's eyes through the two holes that had been cut out. The eyes were wide with surprise and rage. The half-naked stranger lunged toward Ev Bickham, shoving his gun out of the way.

Bickham was thrown off balance. The Phantom pushed him backward into a chair, the arm of which dug deeply into Bickham's back. He exclaimed in pain, grasping for the masked man's arm. He gripped it and pulled him closer, then raised his pistol and brought it down hard on the man's shoulder.

The Phantom emitted an agonized grunt, smashing his elbow with all his force into Bickham's jaw. Bickham's head snapped back sickeningly and he stumbled, his hands reaching clumsily for something to hold on to. He dropped the pistol as he fell backward. The Phantom knelt and snatched the gun by the barrel. He turned it around and pointed it at Bickham, thumbing back the hammer as he did so. Bickham saw the gun pointing directly at him and braced himself for the shot.

Instead there was a loud crash and the Phantom crumpled forward as a chair broke apart over his back. Lucy Bickham stood over him, her hands still on the legs of the chair she had brought from the bedroom. She started to lift the mangled chair in order to hit him again when the Phantom shoved her backward toward the hallway. He dropped the gun and ran for the front door of the cabin. Ev Bickham was almost back on his feet when the man passed him and gave him a hard shove toward the floor. Bickham was on his back when the Phantom tore open the front door and disappeared into the night, his bare legs pale in the moonlight.

★　★　★

An hour later, the Phantom stood in the shadows of a woodpile behind another farmhouse — a house only about two miles from the home of Everett and Lucy Bickham. He was perfectly still, listening for talking or sounds of movement within the home.

He was angry with himself for losing control of the situation at the Bickham's place. It had been dangerous to go in without pants on, but something had compelled him to do it. It had hindered his escape and he promised himself he wouldn't try another stunt like that again.

He was also angry because he had

missed his chance with Lucy Bickham. He had been watching her for over three years, waiting . . . just waiting. She wasn't the prettiest woman around, but there was something very alluring about her, at least in his mind. She had always been friendly to him when they had met around town. He smirked behind his mask. If only she had known who he really was . . .

Now the opportunity was gone, and he hadn't been able to enjoy himself — to make the Bickhams submit to his power, and to fear it. He felt a tinge of bitterness. He would be more cautious. After all, he hadn't spent years planning his return just to throw it all away by taking unnecessary risks.

He looked around the densely forested hillside behind him. Mist laced the gloomy trees. He had picketed his horse a few dozen yards away, just within the rim of the woods.

After ten minutes, he decided that the people in the house were asleep. He stepped around the woodpile and leaned against the back door, then wedged an iron bar into the doorjamb and pushed. The door slid open noiselessly, just as he knew it would. He had been here before, when nobody was home. He had found a way to get inside the house without being detected.

He wouldn't make the same mistakes again. Had he gotten arrogant because, even after all these years, he had never been caught? Not getting caught — that was more important than everything else. He must never, ever be apprehended. The best way to do that was to take control of the situation as quickly as possible. Be merciless. They were much less likely to fight back if they thought he would kill them. Because, if he decided he had to, he would kill them.

He adjusted the mask on his face, removed his pistol from his waistband, and stepped through the back door into the darkened home.

★   ★   ★

Ed Burton had just finished boiling coffee and pouring a cup for Annie when he saw Maynard Blayloch ride out of the trees into his front yard. He put the pot down and carried her cup into the living room, where she sat on the couch with Edith the cat on her lap. She was looking at a yellowed, tattered piece of paper on which a knitting pattern had been scrawled over thirty years ago by her mother and passed down to Annie.

On the table beside her was the photograph of their two boys, who had been dead from scarlet fever for almost a decade now. Burton reminded himself again of why he had quit being a lawman.

'Maynard's here,' he said, handing her the cup. Steam drifted up from it as she took a sip. He saw that she had an anxious expression on her face. She lifted her head and recognized the tension in his expression.

'I hope he's not here because — ' she began.

She hadn't finished her thought when a series of firm knocks resonated from the front door. Burton's face tightened as he stepped across the room and opened the door. Maynard Blayloch, looking distinctly haggard and concerned, removed his hat and nodded politely to Annie Burton, who sat directly across from the door.

'Good morning, Mrs Burton,' he said. 'Mr Burton.'

Burton moved aside and allowed Blayloch to step into the room. The air outside was bracing beneath a gray, cloud-choked sky.

'What's going on, Maynard?' asked Burton.

'The Phantom,' said Blayloch. His tone contained a combination of anger and self-criticism. 'Attacked twice last night. The Bickhams and the Sheeds.'

'Oh, my God,' said Annie quietly. She put her cup down on the table.

'He kill anyone?' asked Burton.

'No, thank God,' said Blayloch. 'Matter of fact, he almost got himself shot by Ev Bickham. Wasn't wearing any pants when he attacked them.'

Burton was incredulous. 'Not wearing any pants?' he asked.

Blayloch nodded slowly. 'He barely made it out the door alive. Lucy broke a chair over his back.'

'Good,' said Annie sharply.

'From there the son of a bitch went to the Sheed farm. Broke in with three little kids in the house.'

'Be damned,' said Ed Burton, shaking his head. 'He hurt the kids?'

'No,' said Blayloch. His relief was obvious.

'Did he do his usual routine?' Burton probed.

'All of it — the ropes, the dishes, everything.' He sighed heavily and Ed Burton urged him to take a seat in a chair in the living room. Burton sat down at the other end of the couch from Annie.

'Who came to you — Bickham or Sheed?' asked Burton.

'Sheed.'

'How'd you find out about Bickham?'

'Sheed told me. The Phantom told Sheed and his wife that he'd been over at the Bickhams' first. They said he was kind of bragging about it.'

'This man is sick,' Annie asserted.

'He smashed Sheed in the head real bad,' Blayloch said. 'Side of his head's all swollen up. Wonder if he was trying to kill him.'

'That wouldn't surprise me,' murmured Burton. He looked across the room toward the deputy sheriff, and he felt concerned for his distress.

Maynard was a very conscientious officer of the law, and this was something that Burton had always respected about him. He hoped Blayloch wasn't in over his head.

'How are you holding up, Maynard?' he asked. 'I know how things like this can consume a man.'

'Ain't that the truth,' said Blayloch with a befuddled shake of his broad head. 'Even when I was in bed last night, all I did was lay there and think about this . . . Phantom. I didn't get any sleep at all — not a wink! That makes two straight nights now.'

'I've been in those shoes,' said Burton sympathetically. 'You need my help with anything?'

Maynard Blayloch was sheepish, but only for a moment.

'Since you asked, I wonder if you'd mind going over to the Sheed place with me. I didn't get much of a chance to talk to them this morning because Mike Sheed went to see the sawbones about his head right after he woke me up. I'd like to have you along in case you think of any questions or see anything that would be useful or that I mightn't think to ask.'

Burton pushed himself to his feet. 'Let me get my coat and my hat and I'm at your service,' he said. He left the room for a few moments.

'Maynard, you're going to get this feller, I just know it,' said Annie.

The deputy grinned crookedly, grateful for the encouragement.

'I sure hope so, ma'am,' he said.

'I don't know how you're going to do it,' she admitted, 'but you'll get him. And don't worry about asking Ed for help. He needs to get out of the house more and he's dealt with this kind of thing more than once. He wants to help you — don't forget that.'

Burton entered the room, shrugging into his sheepskin. He grabbed his Stetson off the nail from which it hung near the front door. He settled it over his mostly bald head and nodded at Blayloch.

'Ready when you are,' he said.

Blayloch rose stiffly and followed Burton to the door.

'Good day, Mrs Burton,' he said.

* * *

Mike Sheed answered the door to his home, his head heavily plastered in bandages. His left eye was blackened and swollen almost shut. There was a grim set to his jaw. This man's spirit isn't broken, thought Burton. He only wants revenge — and who can blame him?

'See you got in and seen the doc, Mike,' said Blayloch. He didn't want to start out with an inappropriately innocuous greeting under the circumstances.

Sheed's eyes were hard. 'Yeah, he patched me up good.'

Blayloch pointed at Burton and said, 'This here's Ed Burton. I think you two know each other. He was a marshal for several years over in the eastern part of our state.'

'Good to see you, Ed,' Sheed said, thrusting his hand forward.

'Wish we weren't getting reacquainted like this.' Burton took Sheed's hand and shook it firmly, as if to reassure the farmer of his friendship. 'I'm going to do everything I can to help Maynard find this feller. He needs to be stopped.'

'That he does,' Sheed said in an even tone.

The interview revealed little that Burton and Blayloch didn't already know. The Phantom had once more followed his typical routine, although this time he had been unusually loquacious, bragging about his escape from the Bickham house.

He had also been exceptionally aggressive, as Sheed's injuries indicated.

They concluded the interview and rode down into town through a light drizzle of rain. They went to Blayloch's office, which was just off Main Street.

Blayloch removed his wet hat and tossed it on to his desk as he sat down. Burton took the seat across the desk from the deputy.

'Any suggestions?' Blayloch asked dejectedly.

Burton turned and watched the rain fall into the muddy street outside. He had spent much of the previous night awake, turning the case over in his mind.

'I think our best bet is to start putting

men out at night to keep a watch for him,' Burton said finally. 'The reason he's been able to get away with this is that once he gets the people tied up, he's in the clear. He can stay as long as he wants and then leave without anyone trying to stop him. But if we have men hidden in the trees, we're bound to catch him roaming around sooner or later.'

Blayloch leaned forward and rested his elbows on the desktop as Burton spoke.

'We should get some men together and get our plan organized by tomorrow night,' Burton said. 'Me, you, and at least one other man who's good with a gun and a horse. Two or three men would be even better.'

'I'll find some men,' Blayloch said.

'We'll have to be in position by midnight tomorrow. He seems to strike mostly after two in the morning, but I think he spends a lot of time just watching the houses before he breaks in. This guy's a planner — he's real careful. He's probably got a bunch of houses already staked out that he could attack on any given night.'

'Like he did when the Bickhams chased him out.'

Burton nodded. 'Like I said — he's a planner. That's how he got away with it the first time 'round. We just have to cut him off at the pass.'

Blayloch was excited, his confidence bolstered by Burton's suggestions.

'I'm going to ask Hank Kirby if he can help out,' he said. 'He can shoot and he can ride, no question about it. He'll be glad to help. Hell, he has a wife and daughters — he doesn't want this Phantom running loose. And I'll do some asking around this afternoon for more volunteers.'

'We have to figure out where to post ourselves. If we're out every night, we'll run into him. We're bound to. He's on a spree right now. He'll be ready to do it again real soon, you can bet on it.'

'I think you're right,' Blayloch said. He squeezed his hands together with tension as he thought about the Phantom.

Burton rubbed his beard. 'I had another idea, too. We need to hold some kind of town meeting to inform the locals that the Phantom is back. People need to know to be vigilant with him on the prowl again.'

'That's a good idea,' Blayloch said. He removed his watch from his pocket and examined it briefly. 'It's just after noon right now. I can spend the afternoon spreading the word about the meeting. When you think we should hold it?'

'As soon as possible. Tonight, if we can.'

'We can,' the deputy said with a grin. His spirits were clearly rising now that a plan was being formed. 'We can use the Episcopal church; I'm good friends with the vicar.'

'That'd be fine,' Burton said.

'I think I'll tell people the meeting starts at seven o'clock.'

Blayloch stifled a yawn. 'You hungry?'

'Getting there.'

'Let's get something to eat before I hit the trail,' Blayloch suggested.

They ate a large meal at a nearby café before Burton left to return home. He agreed to stop by his neighbors' homes and tell them of the meeting.

★　★　★

Blayloch spoke with the local Episcopal priest and quickly gained permission to use the church for the meeting. The clergyman promised to have the church ready by the designated time. Then Blayloch spent nearly five hours riding hard, visiting more than two dozen homesteads, farms, and ranches from Oakridge to Deception Creek. He barely had time to get back to Oakridge before the meeting started.

When Burton rode up to the church it was quite dark out. The air was crisp and a fog was rolling in, as it usually was at that time of the year in this mountainous, heavily forested terrain. The lanterns were bright inside the church and Burton could see a large crowd through the windows. Several horses were tied to the hitching posts outside the church, and at least a dozen wagons and buggies were parked nearby.

Burton climbed the stairs and was reaching for the door handle when Maynard Blayloch opened the door from within.

'Evening, Maynard,' Burton said. 'I see you really spread the word.'

Burton closed the door and surveyed the room. Men, women, and children were everywhere, sitting in pews or standing in small groups, talking amongst themselves. He was pleased to see several of his neighbors among the crowd.

'I didn't have to do much more than tell them the Phantom was back,' Blayloch observed, his face still red and shiny with perspiration after his arduous ride. 'Lot of folks around here are still scared of him.'

'And rightly so.' Burton noticed the elderly vicar emerge from a door behind the altar and look toward him and Blayloch. 'I think he's ready for us to start.'

He followed Blayloch up the aisle between the rows of pews. The priest sat down in a chair near the altar, before which Burton and Blayloch stood. Blayloch gripped his hat nervously.

'Evening, folks,' he began, his voice faltering at first but gaining strength as he spoke. 'I want to thank y'all for coming tonight. I think most everyone knows why we're here.' He glanced around the room. 'Well, just in case you don't know, we're here because the Phantom is back.' There was murmuring through the crowd, although presumably everyone there had already received the news. Burton could sense a genuine fear within the room. The local residents had clearly not forgotten the Phantom's earlier reign of terror.

A man in the front row raised his hand and Blayloch pointed at him.

'I'm sorry,' the man said, looking around apprehensively at all the eyes that had turned toward him. 'I only moved here two years ago. Who is this Phantom character?'

'That's a good question,' Blayloch responded. He was quiet for a moment, thinking about his response. 'The Phantom is a masked rapist who breaks into people's houses in the middle of the night. He holds people at gunpoint and ties them up. Then he . . . violates the woman while her husband is tied up.'

Again the murmur spread across the people like a wave. Blayloch swallowed nervously. Public speaking wasn't his strong suit, but Burton thought he was doing well.

'In the summer of 1874, he carried out four of his attacks, at least that we know of.' His eyes again scanned the faces before him. 'Some of us are pretty sure that he committed more of these heinous acts at that time than just the four we know about.' He hesitated. 'Can't say I blame folks if something like this happened to them and they didn't want to tell the law about it.'

Blayloch ran his fingers through his hair and paused for a time. Then he continued.

'He was gone for five years. Lot of us thought that he maybe moved somewheres, or got sent to jail. Maybe even died. But he's broke into three houses in the last forty-eight hours. He's not just back, he's back with a vengeance. Now the reason I wanted to get everybody together is to make sure y'all are vigilant. Keep a gun right near your bed. Lock all your doors and windows. Keep a lantern lit so he can't sneak up on you in the dark.' Blayloch turned to Burton. 'Marshal Burton, you got anything you'd like to add?'

Burton coughed. 'A few things, yes,' he said. 'First, I don't think this feller ever left Oakridge. I think he's been here the whole time, watching and waiting.' Out of the corner of his eye, Burton could see Blayloch nodding in agreement. 'Why he didn't do this for five years, I don't know. But you got to bear in mind that we think this varmint

48

could end up killing someone. He's mean as a snake. He's told almost all of the victims that he's going to kill them and he's come close once or twice now. I think if he's cornered, he'll do whatever it takes to get away.'

A tired-looking middle-aged man in the second row stood up and spoke. 'Anyone ever got a look at him?'

Blayloch shook his head. 'Not even once. He wears some kind of sack over his head. He seems to be in his twenties or thirties, about average size. Only thing people have seen is his eyes. They're blue, in case you're wondering.'

Burton gestured toward the crowd. 'He could be here right now, in this very room.'

The murmur began again, louder than ever this time. Heads turned as every young man was examined by his neighbors in the pews.

'This Phantom's a right smart feller,' Burton said. 'He watches these folks before he attacks their homes. I'll bet he knows when they come and go. He might even go in the houses when the people are gone. He's real careful.'

A young man at the back of the room rose. 'I just got to say something.'

Blayloch raised a hand for silence, then allowed the young man to speak.

'I just can't believe any grown man would let this little bushwhacker rape his woman in front of him.' Several others nodded in agreement. 'By God, I'd like him to try that on me sometime. I'd blast his ass straight to hell before he knew what hit him.'

The vicar's face flushed with disapproval, as did those of many of the wives and mothers.

Blayloch smiled awkwardly, but Burton was irritated.

'That's all well and good when you're standing here in the church with half the town,' he said. 'When some madman in a mask is holding a pistol in you and your wife's faces and threatening to kill your whole family, the perspective might be a little different.' The young man smirked as Burton went on. 'Lord knows I'd be happy if he breaks into the wrong house and someone is quicker on the draw than he is. That's why you have to be alert. He takes people by surprise.'

The young man sat down. A few men patted him on the back as he did so.

'Marshal Burton is right, everybody,' Blayloch said. 'These people who were attacked — the husbands weren't cowards. Some of these folks had children in the house, too. He promised to kill the kids if he didn't get what he wanted.' Blayloch gave some details of the recent attacks, although he was deliberately vague about who the victims were. He assumed many in the room already knew.

As Blayloch spoke, Burton's attention shifted to a young man standing across the room from him, leaning against a post by the front door. He hadn't noticed him before, but Burton found something about his affect disturbing. The man was of average height and build, clean-shaven with short, dark brown hair. He wore the clothes of a ranch hand, with a large Stetson pulled down low over his face. He was glaring at Blayloch, his mouth set in a sneer of contempt or hatred, or both. He didn't blink as he fixed his hard eyes on the deputy sheriff. Burton had an urge to find out what color his eyes were.

Minutes passed, and still Burton watched the man glare at Maynard Blayloch. Then he abruptly shifted his gaze from Blayloch to Burton himself. Their eyes locked and Burton's heart began to beat faster. He became aware that someone was saying his name, too.

'Marshal Burton?'

Burton turned to Blayloch. He realized that everyone in the room was looking at him.

'Sorry, Maynard,' he said, his face reddening. 'What were you saying?'

'I was just asking if you had anything else you wanted to say about the Phantom . . . '

'Um — did you mention the nightly

patrols we're going to set up?'

'Nope, I plumb forgot.' Blayloch looked back at the crowd. 'Everybody, we're planning on organizing nightly patrols in shifts in and around Oakridge, and as far west as Deception Creek. Figure we're going to need three or four men at a time, along with Marshal Burton and myself. Make it that much harder for the Phantom to play his little games. But that doesn't mean you shouldn't be on guard.'

Burton looked quickly toward the other side of the room. The door was shutting and the man who had been staring murderously at Blayloch was gone. Burton took a step toward the door as Blayloch wrapped up the meeting.

'Before everybody heads home,' the deputy said, 'I'd like to see any man above sixteen years of age. We need as many men on patrol as we can get.'

Burton continued down the aisle as the men in the room moved toward where Blayloch was standing. One man stuck out a hand in greeting to Burton, who smiled quickly and patted the man on the arm without stopping to exchange greetings. The women and children were leaving to wait outside for the men. They formed a large, slow-moving crowd at the door of the church. Burton pushed his way through as gently as he could, finally making it to the doorway and stepping out into the cold night air. His progress had been significantly impeded.

The man was nowhere to be seen. He could have been on a horse and halfway out of town by the time Burton made it out of the church.

Burton waited more than a minute for the crowd to dissipate around the door, then went back in and stood by until Maynard Blayloch had finished writing down men's names and the evenings on which they preferred to participate in the patrols.

'Now, fellers — remember, I'm going to do my best to accommodate your preferences, but I can't make any promises,' Blayloch said. 'The four who volunteered for tomorrow night should meet me outside my office at eleven. We'll need a little extra time to get everybody set up where we want them.' He saw the impatience on the men's faces and concluded quickly, 'All right, men. Thank you kindly. Don't forget to lock all your doors and windows, now, y'hear?'

The men began to disperse and Burton walked up to Blayloch.

'Maynard, did you happen to notice the young man at the back of the room?'

Blayloch knitted his brow. 'Which one?'

'Dark hair, clean shaven. Wearing a big Stetson.'

After a moment, Blayloch remembered. 'Yeah — standing by the door? That guy?'

'Yep, that's him.' There was an urgency to Burton's tone.

'Why, that's Emerson Dodge.'

'You know him?'

'Not real well. He lived here when he

was younger, then left. He just moved back maybe six months ago. His uncle left him a little land a few miles past Deception Creek.'

'Was Buck Dodge his uncle?'

'Yeah, he's Buck's nephew. Buck died just before you and Annie moved back here, if I remember right . . . '

'He was watching you real hard,' Burton pointed out.

'Was he?'

'He was. He have any reason not to like you?'

Blayloch shrugged. 'None I can think of.'

Burton walked over near a window and looked down the street outside. It ran west, leading eventually out of town, through the mountains toward Eugene. That was the direction Emerson Dodge must have ridden.

'You know, I think I'm going to take a little night ride out toward Deception Creek.'

Blayloch raised an eyebrow quizzically. 'That right?' he asked.

'Nothing too important,' Burton said with a nod. 'Just take a little look around.' He looked again out into the foggy blackness of the Oregon night. Apart from a few stragglers, most of the townspeople who had attended the meeting were either gone or in the process of leaving. He turned back to Blayloch. 'I'll be at your office tomorrow night at eleven,' he said. 'If I find anything interesting on my ride tonight, I'll let you know.' He paused. 'You make sure to get some rest. You look real tired, Maynard.'

They shook hands and Burton walked rapidly out of the church and down the steps out front. He untied his horse and pulled its reins in the direction of Deception Creek.

4

About forty-five minutes later, Burton halted on the dark, muddy road and looked down at Deception Creek. It was a glimmering trickle in the moonlight.

A narrow, rutted trail branched off from the main road. There were only a few homes in this area, and Burton was pretty sure he knew where Emerson Dodge lived. He remembered the young man's uncle, a kindly bachelor who owned a few acres tucked in the wooded hills just west of Deception Creek. If Burton was right, this trail led out to the Dodge place. He turned and started up the trail. He took his time, because he remembered the little cabin wasn't far off the road.

He observed the cabin ahead to his right. It was in a small clearing, and a thin wisp of smoke drifted up from the chimney. A lamp was burning behind the smudged, dirty windows, but he couldn't see anyone moving inside.

He sat for about ten minutes, just watching. He assumed someone was in there, although he couldn't be sure given the lack of movement inside. He dismounted and moved his horse several yards into the trees, where he picketed it. He moved stealthily toward the edge of clearing. Some light spilled out from a window in the cabin. Burton was careful to stay in the shadows.

He stopped behind a massive fir, no more than ten feet from the window. He was perfectly still, eyes riveted on the cabin. Another half-hour passed with no sign of life in the small dwelling. Burton knew Dodge could be lying down, or sitting somewhere out of his line of sight. He dared not get closer to confirm one way or another, since doing so would inevitably expose him.

Finally Burton decided he had had enough. He cat-footed back through the trees to his horse, which he led back to the trail. He mounted and rode back to the main road. He turned toward Oakridge.

He had ridden a little over two miles when the rifle sounded. The bullet tossed mud into the air a few feet ahead of Burton. His horse whinnied loudly and side-stepped away from where the bullet had hit. It lifted its front legs and pawed at the air. Burton struggled to stay in the saddle, gripping the reins hard with his left hand while his right moved like lightning toward the Navy Colt strapped to his hip.

He had almost gotten the animal under control when another shot exploded from the darkness of the trees above him. This time the shooter didn't miss. The bullet entered the horse's head just behind its right eye, killing it instantly. Its body collapsed on the ground, tumbling toward its left side as all four legs buckled simultaneously. Burton barely had time to get his leg out of the stirrup before the horse hit the ground.

As the animal fell, Burton used his right leg to push himself away from it. He rolled down an embankment on the far side of the road and took cover behind the base of a tree. His pistol was still in his hand as his eyes scanned the hillside across the road.

The trees were blanketed in darkness. The shooter was up there, hiding and no doubt watching. He must have seen where Burton went after jumping off the falling horse. The moonlight illuminated the area where Burton crouched, but not the hillside opposite him. Burton remained motionless, waiting to see if the shooter would expose himself.

And then he did.

A shot rang out from the hillside, a little to Burton's left. He saw the brief flicker from the end of the barrel as the shooter fired, revealing his position. The bullet hit the tree a few feet above Burton's head, sending bark and woodchips raining down on his hat. He leapt suddenly to his right, raising his pistol and firing three rapid shots toward the location from which the bullet had come.

He heard the sound of sudden, desperate scurrying in the trees where he had fired. The shooter was on the move. Burton knew he hadn't hit him, but evidently he had scared him. The shooter hadn't expected Burton to see the rifle flame and respond so quickly and accurately.

Burton jumped up the embankment and ran past the body of his dead horse. He darted across the road into the trees below the spot where the shooter had launched his ambush. He paused for a moment, listening. He could still hear someone rushing through the foliage above him.

The hunter was now the prey. Burton smiled thinly and continued his pursuit, ignoring the branches that slapped against his face and spectacles.

The shooter had crested the hill and started to descend on the other side. Burton wasn't far behind, but the shooter's lead was sufficient. By the time Burton began making his way down the slope, his quarry had made it to his horse and mounted. Burton could hear the agitated animal's hoofs somewhere below in the trees, moving quickly away on some forest trail. Almost breathless, Burton put his gun back in its holster and paused to lean against a tree. His pulse was pounding and sweat poured down his face.

After a few minutes, he climbed back over the hill and unhitched the saddle on his dead horse. The thick, slippery mud enabled him to push the horse's corpse over the edge of the road into the ravine below. He slung his saddle over his shoulder and began the long walk home.

* * *

It was nearly two in the morning when Burton reached his house. A lantern glowed inside behind the curtains that had been pulled over every window. Annie had waited up for him, as he knew she would.

He tapped on the door, which he knew would be locked. A curtain rustled briefly in a nearby window and then Annie opened the door. He could see a bulge in the pocket of her sweater and knew she was keeping his other Navy Colt close at hand. With the Phantom on the loose, she wasn't going to be caught unawares. Fourteen years as a lawman's wife had taught her that.

'I didn't hear you put your horse in the stable,' she said, a look of concern crossing her face.

'Someone shot my horse out from under me out near Deception Creek,' he said, closing the door and lowering the plank across it. 'Damn near crushed my leg when it fell.'

It was warm in the cabin. He removed his sheepskin and hat and hung them up. He put his arm around Annie and they walked over to the couch. Burton sat down with a groan.

'I've been walking damn near four hours,' he said.

'Who shot your horse?' she asked.

He shook his head. 'I have no idea. But whoever it was, he was shooting to kill. I got off a few shots and must have come real close to his position, because he ran out of there in a hurry.' He leaned forward and removed his boots.

'What were you doing out at Deception Creek?'

'Saw someone at the town meeting who made me suspicious.' He turned toward her. 'You remember Buck Dodge?'

She nodded. 'Haven't seen him in years, though. He must be pretty old by now.'

'He's dead now. Died a little while before we moved back. Anyway, he left his property to his nephew. Kid name of Emerson. I didn't know who he was until Maynard told me. He was standing at the back of the meeting tonight, looking at Maynard like he wanted to slit his throat.'

'Why?' she asked.

'Don't know. I asked Maynard if he

knew why, and he didn't know, either. This Emerson Dodge skipped out real quick at the end of the meeting. I decided to ride out to his property and look around. There was light in the cabin but I didn't see anyone moving around in there. I left after a while and had only gone a mile or two when someone started shooting from the trees up on a hill.'

'Was it this . . . Emerson Dodge?'

'I think it's a distinct possibility.'

'What are you going to do?'

Burton was quiet for a moment, considering the question.

'I'm going to meet with Maynard tomorrow morning,' he said slowly. 'We're going to take a closer look at Emerson Dodge. Maybe even pay him a visit.'

★   ★   ★

Burton's exhaustion was such that Annie let him sleep in late the next morning. She was reading in the living room when she saw the rider burst out of the trees across the yard and move toward the house at a very rapid pace. She got a good look at him when he finally halted in front of the porch. He was a big man, raw-boned and strong, somewhere in his late fifties. She recognized him as Hank Kirby, a local rancher, and opened the door.

'Good morning, Mr Kirby,' she said. She didn't want to sound too cheerful because she could tell that it wasn't good news that brought him to her front door.

Kirby removed his hat. His lined face was somber.

'Good morning, Mrs Burton,' he said quietly. 'Is Mr Burton around?'

'I was just getting ready to wake him up,' she replied. 'Would you like to come in and have a cup of coffee?'

'That's very kind of you, ma'am. But I'm afraid it's rather urgent.'

'I'll get Ed right away,' she said. She moved aside to let Kirby in. 'Please at least come in out of the cold.'

Kirby stepped in and Annie closed the

door. He stood awkwardly as she hurried down the hallway to the bedroom. Burton was snoring softly when she came in and shook him.

'Ed,' she said. 'Wake up. Something's happened.'

Burton's eyes were open almost instantly. He reached for his glasses on the night table and slipped them on.

'What is it?' he asked.

'Hank Kirby is here to see you.'

'Hank Kirby?'

'Yes. He looks real concerned. I think the Phantom might have struck again.'

Burton was already sitting up and looking for his pants before she had finished her last sentence. She returned to the living room as he dressed.

'Mr Kirby, he'll be right out.'

Kirby nodded in thanks. 'Much obliged, ma'am.'

Burton came out of the room about a minute later. He reached out and shook Kirby's hand.

'Hank, how can I help you?' he asked.

Kirby looked nervously toward Annie, as if he didn't feel comfortable discussing the subject in front of a woman. Burton looked from Kirby to Annie, then back to Kirby.

'You can speak in front of Annie. She's heard about a lot of ugly cases.'

'All right then,' Kirby said. 'The Phantom did it again last night. It's real bad.' Kirby's eyes flicked toward Annie and then met Burton's glance. 'He killed them this time. Killed them both.'

The blood drained from Ed Burton's face. 'Who was it?' he asked.

'Bob and Cindy Ballard.'

Burton reached for his coat and hat. 'Let's go,' he said. He walked over and gave Annie a kiss as he shrugged into his sheepskin. 'Don't know when I'll be back.'

'That's fine,' she said, sitting back down on the couch. 'Just make sure to eat.'

It was about a twenty-five minute ride from Burton's front porch to the Ballard place. Burton saddled and rode one of the three horses he still owned, a large, powerful chestnut. Kirby filled Burton in on the way there.

'Cindy's ma came over this morning. The front door was open when she got there. She found Bob and Cindy in their bed.' Kirby swallowed, as if trying to get rid of an unpleasant taste in his mouth. Burton knew the rancher was seeing the image of the dead couple in his mind. 'They both were tied up. Had their heads . . . bashed in.' He shook his head slightly. 'Never seen anything like it. Blood everywhere. I had to take Cindy's ma back home, she was so hysterical. Hell, I practically was, too. On the inside anyway.'

Burton's mind turned to the night before. He was almost sure that it was Emerson Dodge who had taken those shots at him. Was Dodge the Phantom? Had he gone out later, after trying to kill Burton, and killed the Ballards?

Burton put these questions in the back of his mind as he and Kirby rode into the Ballards' yard.

'I live right through those trees,' Kirby said, gesturing behind the house. 'I heard Cindy's ma come out that house screaming like nobody's business. After I saw what happened, I went and got Maynard. He asked me to fetch you.'

They stopped near the front door and tied their horses to the hitching post. Maynard Blayloch stepped out of the house on to the porch. His face showed fatigue and depression.

'Morning, Mr Burton. I guess Hank gave you the details.'

'He did.'

'Well, come on in. Let me tell you, though — it ain't pretty.'

'I'm ready,' said Burton steadily.

Blayloch led the way into the small cabin. Sunlight made the interior bright, but there was a dark, forbidding feeling in the air. Burton had encountered that feeling before on certain murder cases.

They entered the bedroom and Burton was confronted with the bodies of Bob and Cindy Ballard. Blayloch stepped back to a corner of the room and let his colleague take in the scene.

Undoubtedly, this was the work of the Phantom. The man and woman were tied extremely tightly with ropes at both their wrists and ankles. Burton stepped toward the bed and knelt to get a closer look. He had never seen a knot like that before — it was a fancy knot, and clearly a complicated one, in a diamond shape. The hands and feet of both the man and the woman were black from prolonged lack of circulation. Given the tightness of the knots, he guessed their hands had already turned dark purple by the time the killer ended their lives.

Burton rose and stepped back. He had been so interested in the bindings that only now did he take in the full picture. Blood covered most of the wall over the headboard. The blood spatter was mixed with chunks of brain matter and small bits of bone and hair. On the floor near Burton were five or six small dishes, three of which were broken.

He looked down at their heads. The back of both their skulls had been smashed horrifically. Their heads were literally caved in. Cindy Ballard was naked, her face obscured by her long, blood-soaked hair. Bob Ballard was in his underwear. His eyes were open, staring into oblivion.

Blayloch sniffed loudly and gestured to the floor on the other side of the bed from Burton.

'He used this to kill them,' he explained.

Burton stepped around the bed and looked to the floor. There he saw a large piece of chopped firewood, covered in blood and brains. His stomach turned.

'He did it, just like you said he would,' noted Blayloch.

'What's that?' Burton asked, still distracted by the murder weapon.

'He's killing them now. He's not satisfied with just rape anymore.'

Burton let out a heavy sigh. 'He knew that patrols were starting tonight.' He gestured back down the hallway. 'Let's go out front and talk. I've seen enough.'

The sun was in their eyes as they stepped out into the yard. Blayloch turned to Kirby.

'Hank — do you think you could ride out to Bob's brother's place and let him know?'

Without hesitating, Kirby put a boot in a stirrup and mounted his horse. 'I'll take care of that, Maynard.' He rode across the yard and disappeared into the trees.

Blayloch looked at Burton and said, 'Good man, Hank Kirby.'

Burton nodded sincerely. Blayloch took a deep breath and rubbed his hand down his unshaven face, pawing it out of shape. The bags under his eyes were pronounced.

'Well, this is a hell of a thing, ain't it?' he asked Burton. He took off his hat and scratched at the back of his head.

'Yes, it is,' said Burton deliberately. 'No question about that.'

'I guess the only thing we can do

right now is hope the nightly patrols either smoke him out or make him scared to try it again.'

Burton was silent for a spell, looking off into the grass.

'I reckon you're right, Maynard,' he said. 'This feller is smart, but he's also got a lot of sand. I don't think he's going to stop because of the patrols. If anything, that'll probably provoke him — make him want to show how smart he is, and how stupid we are. That's when he'll make a mistake.'

Blayloch looked up. 'You think so?' he asked.

'I'm fairly sure of it. This is some sort of strange obsession for him. He's got something to prove now.'

'To who?'

Burton shrugged. 'Don't know. Maybe the law, maybe himself.' He glanced at Blayloch. 'I have to tell you what happened last night after the meeting.'

'What's that?' Blayloch asked eagerly.

'I went out and took a look at Buck Dodge's old place.'

'Yeah?'

'Yep. The lamp was lit and the chimney was smoking, but I didn't see anybody in there, and I was watching the place for more than an hour.'

'So what happened?'

'I ended up leaving Deception Creek and had gone a couple miles back toward Oakridge when some bush-whacker shot at me with a rifle. He killed my horse.'

'I'll be damned,' Blayloch said, obviously alarmed.

'He wasn't out to scare me,' Burton said. 'He was out to kill me. I got some shots off at him and scared him away. Chased him up the hill but he had a head start on me and got to his horse before I could catch him, or get a look at him.'

Blayloch's eyes were wide. 'You think it was Emerson Dodge?' he asked.

'Can't say for sure, of course,' Burton said. 'But I can't think of anyone else it could be.'

'We can go have a word with him

after Hank gets back. I'm going to talk to Bob's brother and see that everything gets taken care of here.' He glanced back toward the open front door of the house. 'Damn shame,' he said sadly. 'Bob and Cindy were good people. Yeah, Bob was a bit of a loudmouth and drank too much, but he wasn't a bad feller.' He squinted in the sun. 'You remember what he said at the town meeting last night?'

Burton frowned. 'What's that? He was there?'

'Yeah, sure he was,' Blayloch said. 'He's the one who stood up and said he'd like to see the Phantom try to rape his wife. He said he'd kill him rather than submit.'

The hair stood up on the back of Burton's neck. 'That was Bob Ballard?'

'Sure was.'

'Son of a bitch,' Burton said. 'Didn't recognize him in . . . that state. So he was there.'

'Yeah, you put him in his place, remember?'

'No, no,' Burton said impatiently. 'The Phantom. He was there, at the meeting.'

Blayloch looked slightly surprised, as if he had thought the Ballards had been chosen randomly. 'Hmmm,' he said. 'I guess he was.'

'He took Bob Ballard's big talk as a challenge,' Burton remarked. 'And he decided to take the challenge.'

'I'll be damned!' Blayloch said again.

They didn't speak for a while, both lost in thought. When Ballard's brother finally returned with Hank Kirby, Blayloch had the unpleasant task of explaining the situation to him. Mike Bonham took the information as stoically as Burton could imagine, although the strain and horror were etched across the young man's face. Eventually other family members began to arrive, and then some neighbors came over to help as best they could.

An hour later, Burton and Blayloch rode out of the Ballards' yard. They headed toward Emerson Dodge's place.

5

When they reached Deception Creek, Ed Burton and Maynard Blayloch turned left off the main road and began riding toward the Dodge property.

'My pa was friends with Buck Dodge,' Burton said.

'Mine, too.'

The elder Dodge had been a fixture in the Oakridge area for decades before his death the year before.

'They used to go hunting together in those hills there beyond the edge of the homestead,' Blayloch noted. He pointed to the misty peaks in the distance. 'Ever been out there?'

Burton shook his head.

'There are a couple of caves up there. A man could live in them. We used to stay three or four days up there.'

When Burton and Blayloch halted in Emerson Dodge's yard, they noticed the front door of his cabin was wide open. They dismounted and picketed their horses. They heard some kind of activity going on behind the house and were about to walk back and take a look when the sounds ceased and Dodge came around the corner.

He was covered in blood, from head to toe. Burton and Blayloch stopped in their tracks, Blayloch's hand reaching down toward the holster on his hip. Burton's hand didn't move.

'You stop right there, Emerson,' Blayloch said. 'Put your hands up.'

Dodge stopped and raised his hands. He glared at the two men standing before him.

'You got a reason to be here?' he snarled.

'You got a reason for being covered in blood like that?' Burton retorted.

'What's it to you?' Dodge said.

'We found two bodies in a cabin this morning,' Burton said. 'Their heads were crushed. It was pretty bloody, as you can imagine.'

Dodge sneered. 'And you think I did it?' He snorted with contempt.

'Answer the question,' Blayloch said. 'Why you got all that blood on you?'

'I went hunting this morning. Got me a big old buck. Been gutting and dressing it for the last hour.'

Burton and Blayloch exchanged skeptical glances.

Turning back to Dodge, Burton said, 'Then you won't mind if we go around back and take a look.'

Dodge frowned and wiped his palms on the sides of his pants. 'This is my property. I got the papers for it. It's all legal. You ain't got no right to be coming around and harassing me.'

'We're investigating some killings,' Burton said steadily. 'You'd be wise to cooperate.'

Dodge chewed on a plug of tobacco in his cheek, his eyes locked on Burton's.

'Are you even a lawman?' he asked disdainfully.

'Mr Burton is acting in an . . . un-official capacity on this case,' said

Maynard Blayloch.

Dodge laughed. 'Whatever the hell that means . . . ' he muttered.

Burton took a step toward Emerson Dodge, who stepped in front of him and put a hand out to block his path toward the back of the cabin. Dodge put his other hand on Burton's sternum and shoved him back roughly.

'Hey!' Blayloch exclaimed.

Burton looked over his shoulder at the deputy. 'Don't worry, Maynard,' he said. 'I can handle this.'

He turned back toward Dodge and stepped forward. When Dodge attempted to block him again, Burton grabbed Dodge's wrist and pulled the homesteader close to him in one very fast movement. Before Dodge could respond, Burton brought up his right arm and drove his elbow hard into the man's throat, then shoved him back. He hooked his right boot behind Dodge's feet as he pushed. Dodge's legs came out from under him and he tumbled backward into the mud, clawing at his throat and gasping for breath.

His face was a deep crimson.

'Let's just call that a warrant,' Burton said, looking down at Dodge. 'Now we're going to take a look around back. Let us know if you have any questions.'

With Blayloch following, Burton stepped around the wheezing man and circled to the back of the cabin. A large deer carcass was dangling there from a hook near the back door, and there was a lot of blood in the area. Dodge's explanation for his bloody state was plausible enough, Burton thought reluctantly.

Blayloch's face showed disappointment. 'Don't mean he didn't kill the Ballards, too,' he asserted.

Burton nodded. 'True.'

They turned and walked back around the cabin. Dodge was on his feet now, crouching over with his hands on his knees. He still struggled to catch his breath. He looked up at Burton and Blayloch with eyes filled with hatred.

'You sons of bitches — you'll pay for this,' he said. 'We got laws in this country.'

'You made this harder than it had to be, Dodge,' Blayloch said with an edge to his tone. 'A little cooperation goes a long way.'

Dodge stood up straight now, his right hand rubbing his throat where Burton had struck him. 'Who the hell you think you are?' he asked Burton, who stared back at him impassively.

'I don't like you, Dodge,' said Burton. 'I think you got something to hide.' He noticed that Emerson Dodge had blue eyes.

'Like what?'

'I don't know yet. But me and Maynard are going to find out. You can bet on that.'

'If you're trying to pin this on me — ' Dodge began.

Blayloch cut him off. 'Nobody's trying to pin anything on you. If you're innocent, then you got nothing to worry about.'

'Yeah, sure.' Dodge looked back and forth between Burton and Blayloch. 'Get out of here. You saw the buck.'

'Fair enough,' Blayloch said. 'I got a couple more questions, though.'

Dodge was irritated. 'Ask 'em, then.'

'Where were you last night?'

'I was at the town meeting.'

'No, *after* the meeting.'

'I was here,' Dodge said, jutting his chin toward the cabin.

'You sure about that?'

'Why wouldn't I be?'

'Don't know,' Blayloch said casually. 'Sometimes people forget things. Especially when it's convenient for them.'

'Well, I ain't forgot nothing. I was here.'

'All night?'

'All night.'

Blayloch sighed. 'You got any more questions, Marshal?' he asked Burton.

'Marshal?' cried Dodge. 'You said yourself he ain't a lawman.'

'Not anymore,' Burton said softly.

'He's solved a lot of murders,' Blayloch said.

Emerson Dodge scoffed.

'I do have one question,' Burton stated.

'Ask it then!' Dodge said, crossing his arms.

'You planning on taking part in the night time patrols?'

Dodge smiled. 'Sure I am.'

'That's good to hear,' said Blayloch.

'You two think I'm the Phantom, don't you?'

'Don't know,' Blayloch replied. 'But if you are, we'll find out.' He remembered something and turned back to Dodge. 'By the way, you used to live around here before, didn't you, Emerson?'

Dodge smirked. 'Before when?'

'When you were younger. Didn't you and your pa live for a while with Buck?'

'Yeah, we did. What about it?'

'When was that?'

After thinking for a moment, Dodge said, 'About five years back.'

Blayloch glanced at Burton, then back to Dodge. 'So it was 1874, then, right? Just to be precise.'

'Yeah — 1874. Like I asked, what of it?'

Blayloch tapped his finger against his temple. 'Just want to get everything straight up here, you know what I mean?'

Dodge said nothing as the two men walked back to their horses. He watched them mount and ride off into the trees toward the road. Then he turned and went back to butchering his deer.

★ ★ ★

The mood was notably somber when the designated patrolmen gathered in Maynard Blayloch's office at eleven o'clock that night. A heavy rain lashed against the windows and the roof.

Blayloch sat on the edge of his desk, a lantern beside him with the wick turned down. Four men sat in wooden chairs in front of the deputy. Ed Burton was one of them.

'I reckon I don't need to tell anyone about what we found this morning,' Blayloch said carefully. 'I think it shows that this Phantom is more of a danger to the good people of this community than some of you may have thought. We got two dead people now, to go along with those who have been attacked by the Phantom and got out alive. Killing's probably what he's been wanting to do all along.' He rubbed his weary eyes for a moment. 'Anyway, these patrols ought to make a big difference. With the five of us spread out, he'll have a hard time travelling in the immediate Oakridge area without one of us spotting him. Hell, this ain't a big town.'

Oakridge could barely be even be *called* a town, thought Burton. It was an isolated little hamlet, deep in the massive Oregon forests about forty miles east of Eugene. Last Burton had heard, the town had an official population of eighty-four residents, not including the twenty or so homesteads and ranches in the area as far as Deception Creek. To date, the Phantom had struck very close to the town. In his attacks from five years before he had even struck *in* town once, at the home of the local printer. The printer and his family moved away from Oakridge within a week of the home invasion. There hadn't been a printing establishment in the town since.

'Remember that these patrols is meant to deter him at least as much as catch him. He may not try his tricks if he knows we're out and about, keeping an eye out for him. Then again, he may try it even though we're patrolling, just to teach us a lesson. If you see him running around in that mask of his, then shoot to kill.'

The man sitting next to Burton shifted in his seat. 'Uh, Maynard — what if we see someone who matches the description but ain't wearing a mask?'

Blaylock thought for a moment. 'Well, I guess you can stop them and ask to see inside their saddle-bags and pockets. Hell, we might just open up a saddle-bag and find the mask in there.' He raised an eyebrow in Burton's direction. 'What do you think, Mr Burton?'

Burton sat up a little straighter. 'I think that'd be all right,' he said. 'People might complain, but . . . just say it's voluntary. They don't have to open their bags or coats if they don't want to.'

'Right!' Blayloch said. 'And let's only ask to check if it's a young man, average build, blue eyes — you got the idea.'

The men nodded.

Blayloch was just about to add something else when a series of loud and insistent knocks on his office door interrupted him. Burton was the closest to the door, so he rose and opened it. A momentary shock went through him as Emerson Dodge stepped into the office out of the pounding rain. Maynard Blayloch's eyebrows shot up in surprise.

'I'm here to help out with the patrols,' Dodge said. There was an unmistakable hostility to his presence, and none of the other volunteers greeted him.

'That's fine,' Blayloch said simply. 'We need all the help we can get.'

The deputy explained how the men were to be distributed. Three would be in town, patrolling different areas. Two would roam the hills west of town where the ranches and homesteads were, and one would patrol the sparsely populated few miles to the east of Oakridge. No one's designated geo-graphical area overlapped with that of another. Blayloch assigned the area to the west to himself and Emerson Dodge, who looked chagrined at the choice. Burton took the job as the sole patrolman east of town. He was the only one of the six men in the office who lived there.

By midnight, the riders were in position. The signal for any trouble was three rapid gunshots in the air. Given the relatively small distances between each horseman, it wouldn't take long for reinforcements to arrive if someone encountered the Phantom.

Burton took the road leading out of town and stayed on it for roughly two miles. Then he turned around and slowly made his way back, stopping in and taking a look at various neighbors' lands to see if he found anything suspicious. He and Blayloch had warned the others not to patrol too close to houses and cabins. The tense atmosphere in town after dark had led to some trigger-happy talk. No one wanted to see someone get shot in the dark by an old homesteader because the latter thought the Phantom was creeping in the shadows outside. The men were on six-hour shifts. Blayloch would have liked to have shorter watch shifts but was unable to do so given the lack of residents in the Oakridge area.

The first evening passed slowly and uneventfully. The only people out on the muddy streets at that time of night were a couple of the town's regular drunks, trying to find their way home. They lived together in a shack on the eastern edge of town and Burton watched them stumble out of the saloon and slowly make their way toward him. They greeted him jubilantly in the moonlight,

and he nodded and smiled in acknowledgement.

★ ★ ★

The six patrolmen met up a little before
six o'clock outside Blayloch's office. It
was still at least an hour until dawn.
It had drizzled lightly but relentlessly
throughout the night. The men were all
cold and tired.

'Well, maybe the patrol made a
difference tonight, men,' said Blayloch,
dismounting. He tied his horse's reins
to the hitching post. 'Thanks for your
help. There'll be another patrol tonight,
but as I said earlier we won't plan on
using any of y'all until a week from
now.' He grinned sardonically. 'That is,
unless you want to volunteer for duty
between now and then.'

A couple of the men forced tired
smiles.

'All right, then — head on home.
Make sure to lock your doors and
windows at night!' He made a vague

waving gesture with his hand and turned to open the front door of his office. He went in as the men turned their horses toward their respective homes and rode away.

Emerson Dodge flicked a glance toward Burton before they separated. Burton met his eyes. He could see the loathing and suspicion in the man's face. A smile creased the corners of Burton's lips.

'You make sure to lock up real careful at night, Mr Dodge, y'hear?' he said.

Dodge looked like he was going to say something in reply, but thought better of it. He turned his horse toward Deception Creek and rode out of town.

* * *

The patrols worked.

Weeks and then months passed without any sign of the Phantom. Seven nights per week, men rode the streets and hills in and around Oakridge.

Maynard Blayloch was especially indefatigable, patrolling at least six nights every week — sometimes seven. He existed on roughly two hours of sleep per night for more than half a year. Sometimes he made up for it with cat naps in his office. Burton had to implore the deputy to take a night off every now and then.

Despite his chronic fatigue, Blayloch was also fairly exuberant much of the time. Annie Burton found this concerning, but her husband knew what Blayloch was going through. The sheer relief Blayloch felt as one day led into another without another home invasion, rape, or murder seemed to be feeding his sometimes manic moods. Well, that combined with the prolonged sleeplessness.

After almost seven months of nightly patrols, pressure from the residents of Oakridge finally led Blayloch to call them off. The men were complaining about the demands on their time, which they said would be unsustainable when spring came and their commitments to working their land increased. Blayloch and Burton warned of what might come were the patrols to be cancelled, but the pressure eventually became too great and one Monday morning in late April the last patrol concluded.

Ed Burton and Maynard Blayloch braced themselves for a new wave of attacks from the Phantom. But nothing happened. Spring gave way to summer, and then autumn came, but still there was so sign of the Phantom. Had he moved away in the face of the nightly patrols? Burton thought it was possible, although somehow he doubted it.

By the time November arrived it had been a year since the last attack. Most folks, it seemed, had either forgotten about the Phantom or no longer feared him.

6

It was a cold, foggy November morning when Ed and Annie Burton encountered Maynard Blayloch outside the general store in Oakridge. Since the end of the patrols, Burton hadn't seen the deputy very often. He was glad to observe that Blayloch appeared much more rested than he had in previous months.

'Maynard, good to see you,' said Burton.

The men shook hands.

Blayloch tipped his hat at Annie. 'Good morning, ma'am. You two keeping warm out there at the cabin?'

'Oh, yes,' Annie responded. 'Ed keeps busy chopping firewood.'

'Well, you two have that big old fireplace. You can probably keep the whole house warm with it.'

'Pretty much,' Burton said. There

were many things he liked about inheriting Annie's father's house, but the massive stone fireplace ranked near the top in Burton's estimation.

'You two keep talking,' Annie said. 'I'm going in.'

She smiled at Blayloch and entered the store, leaving Burton and the deputy alone on the steps outside.

'It'll be one year since the last attack here in a few days,' Burton noted. 'I guess the patrols really did scare him off. They've been over damn near six months and he still hasn't made a move.'

Blayloch blew out his cheeks and shook his head with a thin smile.

'Whatever it is that's keeping him from doing it, I hope it keeps working.' He pushed his hat back on his head and looked into the distance abstractedly. 'Maybe he moved on.'

'That could be,' Burton said. 'There's a very good chance he was doing the patrols with us.'

'You think?'

Burton nodded. 'Only four or five men in this area weren't able to take part in the patrols. I don't think any of those fellers matched the Phantom's description.' He watched Annie through the window of the store where she was perusing a rack of books. She invariably bought three or four whenever the store had some in stock. He turned back to Blayloch. 'I haven't seen Emerson Dodge around in a few weeks.'

'Me, neither,' Blayloch said. 'I heard he was spending some time up in Salem at his brother's place. I'm still keeping an eye on him whenever he's around, though.'

'I would, too, if I were in your boots.'

A homesteader and his family passed by in a wagon and both Burton and Blayloch smiled and waved in greeting. Afterwards they were silent for a minute or two. Life seemed to have returned to a state of normality around Oakridge.

Annie came out of the store with her books. Blayloch saw her and patted Burton on the shoulder.

'I'll let you two get along,' he said. 'Let me thank you again for all the help you gave me.' He turned his eyes to Annie. 'Ma'am, you have yourself a nice day.' He gestured toward the books in her hands. 'Those should keep you busy for a while!'

The Burtons laughed and climbed into their buggy. With a final wave to Maynard Blayloch, they headed back toward their home.

* * *

The Phantom stood behind the tree, watching. He had been doing that his entire life, he thought. Watching, planning, waiting.

The cabin was about thirty yards away. He could see it clearly in the moonlight. No lanterns were lit inside. Most of the curtains were closed, although he could see right into the living room.

It had been almost a year. The desire to attack again had gnawed at him terribly throughout those passing months.

The patrols made that impossible, however. He had at times found it amusing to be patrolling the dark streets, looking for . . . himself.

He had chosen to be disciplined. The only times he had ever come close to being captured or killed in his attacks were when he had chosen to be undisciplined. He had waited for five years; he could wait out the patrols. And he did.

But now he could contain it no longer. He desired to feel again that rush, that incomparable, almost godlike sensation that came when he gained total control over another human being. The impulse was too powerful for him to resist, even had he wanted to, which he didn't anymore.

His pulse was rapid, his senses alert with anticipation. It was like scratching an itch, he thought. He was finally going to satisfy the insistent urge within himself. He was going to make them pay for the year he had spent dormant, biding his time.

He stepped out from behind the tree and stood at the edge of the forest. His breathing was faster now, his eyes riveted on the house . . .

*   *   *

Burton fell asleep early that night, after eating far too much dinner. He kept dozing in bed while trying to read a novel, but finally he surrendered to the inevitable, removed his glasses, and rolled over to sleep. Annie was still awake, reading one of her new books by the light of the lamp on her bedside table.

When Burton awoke hours later, Annie was asleep. The house was immersed in darkness, although he could see moonlight shining on the trees outside through a small gap in the curtains. He lay thinking about nothing in particular for a few minutes and then realized he needed to urinate, and badly.

He rolled out of bed quietly and

crept into the hallway toward the back door. When he opened it, he shivered in the cold night air. He decided not to make the trek across the yard to the outhouse. Instead, he stood on the top step outside the door and relieved himself in the grass off to the side of the house, his teeth chattering uncontrollably by the time he finished. He stepped quickly back through the door and closed it. He continued to shiver, although he regained some measure of control over his teeth.

He moved down the hallway into the living room and approached the fireplace. There were only embers in it now, glowing feebly. He built up a new fire and stood near it for several minutes, warming his frigid limbs. He was just about to walk back down the hallway to his bedroom when his peripheral vision caught some sort of movement in the shadows outside.

Burton froze momentarily, then backed away from the fireplace into a dark corner of the room. He never took his eyes away from the place in the trees across the yard where he had seen something move.

After a few seconds, he saw it again. A shadowy human form had moved there, rustling a large tree branch. Burton squinted through his glasses. He held his breath without being conscious of doing so.

Then the branch shifted once more and a person stepped forward from behind the tree. A cold shock snaked down Burton's neck as the moonlight revealed a man in a burlap mask with holes cut out for the eyes — eyes that seemed to be staring across the dark yard and through the living room window directly at Burton himself.

The passing seconds felt like an eternity as Burton's mind raced. Was the Phantom staring at him? He moved a little to his right, deeper into the darkness on the far side of the fireplace. The Phantom's gaze didn't follow his movements, and Burton concluded that the killer hadn't spotted him. He began to breathe again, albeit shallowly.

Logs crackled in the fireplace. Burton barely heard the sound over the roar of his heartbeat in his ears.

The Phantom shifted on his feet, his eyes still taking in the cabin, hunting for any sign of movement within. Finally he walked rapidly across the yard toward the back of the house and disappeared from sight.

Instantly Burton was in motion. He raced toward the bedroom and grabbed the Navy Colt from his bedside table.

'Annie,' he whispered loudly. 'Annie!'

She rolled over and looked at him with concern on her face.

'The Phantom is outside.' Her eyes widened in horror at his words. He reached into a corner behind his night stand and pulled out a shotgun. It was already loaded. 'Take this,' he said, handing the weapon to Annie.

She took it from him and got out of bed.

'I'm going to meet him at the back door,' Burton said, moving across the room toward the hallway. He didn't need to say anything further to Annie about the situation. She knew her way around a shotgun and wasn't afraid to use it if she had to.

He turned off the hallway into the small, dark passage that led to the back door. Adrenaline flowed through him and he could feel sweat dripping down his back. He stood with his back to the wall, watching the door and waiting.

Burton tensed as a scraping sound came through from the other side of the door. He raised the pistol. The sound continued and then was replaced by the sound of wood creaking, as if the Phantom were using a tool to pry the door open. Then the door moved inward, ever so slightly.

Burton's finger lay against the trigger.

Seconds passed, and then a full minute. Still the door didn't move any further. Burton began to wonder if the Phantom had moved around the house to use the front door instead. Another minute went by. The tension swelled within Burton, whose heart was pounding so hard it seemed like it would burst through his ribcage. After another minute, he took a step back and looked down the hallway toward the living room.

At that moment the back door burst inward toward him. A gust of freezing air hit his face at the same time, and he turned to see the shape of the Phantom in the doorway, no more than six feet away from the spot where Burton stood. The moonlight was bright behind the masked man, who took two rapid steps into the dark hallway before he stopped short.

Burton pivoted again to the back door just as the Phantom stepped inside. He raised his pistol and fired without aiming. The shot missed the Phantom's head by mere inches, exploding into the log wall nearby and sending shards of wood on to his shoulder. The killer released a strangled scream and lunged backward. He vanished through the doorway before Burton could get another shot off.

'Ed?' Annie Burton cried from the bedroom.

'I'm going after him!' he yelled to her. 'You keep that shotgun handy!'

'Oh, thank God,' he heard her cry as he reached the doorway.

He paused for a moment before leaning forward to look around. He saw the man in the mask to his right, running quickly toward the rim of the trees. Still barefoot and wearing only his long john underwear, Burton leapt from the back porch and raced after him.

Burton had made it halfway across the yard when the Phantom reached the trees. By the time Burton entered the forest he could see his quarry running a few dozen yards ahead of him. He could hear branches snapping under the man's feet and slapping hard against his body as he ran.

Burton continued the pursuit, his face and torso lashed by the branches.

Tree roots, fallen limbs, rocks, and pine cones raked across his feet; soon the soles were torn and bloody. A branch knocked his glasses off his face once and he stopped for a moment to pick them up and slip them back on before pushing on. Having thwarted the Phantom and come this close to catching him, Burton's mind was focused solely on the task at hand; he wasn't even aware of the searing pain in his feet or the blood that came close to making him slip and fall three or four times. He could still hear the Phantom's frantic movements through the trees ahead of him. Occasionally he caught a glimpse of the man's shoulders and the back of his hooded head.

The Phantom was steadily increasing his lead on Burton. They approached the edge of a steep incline, where the trees were less dense. Burton was now limping, blood flowing freely from the soles of his feet. He could see the Phantom much more clearly now. He was wearing a white shirt and dark brown pants. Suddenly the killer halted and pivoted toward Burton, kneeling and aiming his pistol at his pursuer. Burton dove to the side just as he fired. The last thing he remembered was the sound of the bullet passing within inches of his head. Then his skull slammed into the wide base of a tree and he was enveloped in total darkness.

Burton wasn't sure how long he was unconscious. When he came to he could feel an intense, throbbing pain on the right side of his head, just above his ear. His wire-rimmed glasses lay on a tree root nearby, the lenses reflecting the moonlight. He picked them up and inspected them. They were bent slightly and he straightened them out and put them on. He looked through the trees toward the incline toward which the Phantom had been racing. There was nothing but stillness and silence in the cold autumn night.

He reached up and felt the injured area on his head. It was swollen and painful but there was surprisingly little blood. From the way the blood had dried, however, he figured he had been out for quite a while. His feet, on the other hand, were torn to bloody shreds. He cursed himself for chasing the Phantom while barefoot. The sight of the rapist and killer in the flesh, preparing to attack him and Annie, had compelled him to act hastily. He pushed himself slowly to his feet and began to hobble back in the direction of his house, cursing with every other step.

It took him nearly a half hour to get home. He yelled Annie's name as he limped across the yard. She appeared at the back door, still holding the shotgun.

'What happened?' she exclaimed.

'Bastard outran me,' he said.

She looked down at his feet. 'What did you do to yourself?'

Burton waved his hand impatiently.

'Just get me some rags and I'll wrap my feet,' he said. 'I've got to get into town and get ahold of Maynard.'

He stepped up on to the back porch. Annie reached out and helped steady him with her hand. He sat down on the porch and she noticed the swollen lump on the side his head.

'Your head!' she cried.

'It's barely bleeding,' he said. 'Now please — bring me some clothes and my boots, after you bring me some rags. I don't want to walk in there and get blood all over your pretty floor.'

She didn't smile at his half-hearted attempt at a joke. Within twenty-five minutes, Burton was dressed, armed, and ready to ride into Oakridge. He had just finished saddling his horse when Annie came back out of the house.

'You're not going to make it far with your feet in that condition,' she said mournfully.

He gave her a kiss on the cheek and mounted his horse.

'Lock up and close the curtains. I don't think he'll be back, but in case he does . . . '

She interrupted him. 'If he does, he'll wish he hadn't.'

Burton nodded, turned his horse toward town, and touched spurs to the animal's flanks.

★   ★   ★

As Burton rode toward Maynard Blayloch's house, his mind hurriedly assessed the events of the night. There were only a few days left before the one-year anniversary of the last attack. What had brought the Phantom back out of the shadows? Why had he chosen the Burtons? His thoughts turned back to Emerson Dodge. He wondered if the homesteader had come back from visiting his relatives in Salem. Then he wondered if Dodge's absence really was because of a trip to his brother's place. It was possible that he had never actually left the area — that he had been lurking around the countryside near Oakridge, planning his next attack. Burton was sure the Phantom watched people's homes before striking. He might have been watching the Burtons' home for days, waiting until he decided it was the right moment to attack.

Burton urged his horse forward on the trail to the main road toward town. Within three minutes he had made it there. He turned left and raced toward Oakridge. The moon hovered above him in the black heavens, and a thick mist sifted its way through the trees on either side of him. He was cold despite his sheepskin coat. His head still throbbed, but he had so much adrenaline flowing through his veins that he was barely conscious of it. But his feet were killing him. The rags with which he had wrapped his feet had very quickly become blood-soaked. As he reached the edge of town, he forced himself to ignore the pain.

He could see the drunkards' shack up ahead on his right. He rode past it down Main Street, heading west. He turned off on to a rutted trail that led into the hills just north of town. He rode for nearly a half a mile and then turned left into the yard of Maynard

Blayloch's cabin. The house was completely dark.

Burton stepped gingerly down from the saddle and tied the reins to a post near Blayloch's front door. He winced as he climbed the steps, then pounded hard on the door. He could hear the deputy's horse snorting and shuffling in the small barn to the side of the house.

Receiving no response, Burton hammered his fist against the door. At last he heard movement within.

'Who's there?' said Blayloch.

'Maynard, it's me — Ed Burton.'

He heard the sound of Blayloch removing the plank from the door. The lawman stepped out into the night air.

'What's wrong?' he asked anxiously.

'The Phantom,' Burton said. 'I caught him trying to break in my house tonight.' Blayloch's eyes widened. 'He might have got in, too, if I hadn't gotten up to piss. I damn near got him with a shot to the head in the hallway at the back of the house. I chased him more than a half a mile. I ended up knocking myself out trying to avoid one of his bullets.' Burton shook his head slightly, still stunned by the turn of events that had unfolded over the last few hours.

'Here, come on in,' said Blayloch. 'I'll throw on some clothes.'

Burton followed him in and watched him light a lantern in the small living room. Blayloch lived in the same home in which he had been born. Despite its bachelor owner, the cabin was fairly tidy. Blayloch walked down the hallway to the first of two bedrooms. Burton could hear him dressing hurriedly.

'Did you get a look at him?' Blayloch called from the bedroom.

'No,' Burton said. 'He had the mask on the whole time.'

Blayloch came back into the living room, pulling his coat over his shoulders. He grabbed his Stetson off a table and planted it on his head. When he looked at Burton, his face was drawn.

'You thinking what I'm thinking?' he asked.

'Emerson Dodge?'

Blayloch's mouth spread into a tight grin. 'We're thinking the same thing.'

'I've had a bad feeling about that feller since the first time I laid eyes on him,' Burton said.

'He's awful squirrely,' Blayloch recalled. 'Of course, that doesn't mean he's the Phantom, but that much hostility does make a man wonder.' Blayloch leaned over and slipped his boots on. 'Let's head on out to his place and see if he's back from Salem.'

'Let's do it,' Burton said, his tone clipped. His desire to apprehend the Phantom was now intense. He had an inkling of what the victims had gone through, both those who had lived and those who had perished. A vision of himself and Annie flashed through his mind — their hands and feet were bound, their heads crushed in, their blood and brain matter festooned across the wall above their bed.

He put the thought out of his head as he mounted his horse. Maynard Blayloch led his own horse out of the barn after saddling it. He swung up atop the animal and nodded toward Burton. Within a few minutes the men were out on the main road, heading west toward Deception Creek.

7

Ed Burton and Maynard Blayloch drew reins about a hundred yards from Emerson Dodge's cabin. They sat in silence, watching. Burton raised a finger and pointed toward the thin wisp of smoke rising from the chimney. Blayloch had seen it, too.

'You want to take the back?' the deputy asked.

Burton nodded. They moved into the trees nearby and picketed their horses. Then they split up, Blayloch creeping toward the front door as Burton slipped around and took up position near the woodpile near the back.

He looked through a grimy window beside the door. He could see no movement within the cabin.

Maynard Blayloch's loud knocks reverberated through the front door.

'Emerson Dodge!' Blayloch called in

a booming voice. 'Come out if you're in there. This is Maynard Blayloch.'

Silence followed. Blayloch's fist pounded on the door.

'Dodge! We know you're in there. Open up!'

After another minute, Burton heard Blayloch's footsteps approaching. He walked back around the woodpile and met the deputy.

'I'm going to check the barn,' Blayloch said.

Burton nodded and waited while Blayloch crossed over to the little barn near the trees. He watched him enter the shadowy structure and then quickly exit and walk back toward the cabin.

'He's in there,' Blayloch said quietly. 'His horse is in the barn — along with another horse.'

'Two people in the cabin?' Burton asked.

'Looks like it,' Blayloch confirmed. He stepped past Burton and looked toward the back door. 'What do you suggest?'

Burton opened his mouth to answer

but, before he could utter a word, the back door was ripped open from inside and a shadowy figure emerged, gun raised and pointed at Blayloch.

'Maynard, get down!' Burton yelled.

Blayloch turned quickly toward the back door.

The words came too late. A deadly flame burst from the barrel of the gun, only about six feet away from the deputy. Blayloch groaned and clutched his chest before collapsing on to the ground.

Burton stepped backward, taking shelter behind the woodpile. His Navy Colt was in his hand and it flashed twice in rapid succession. The man near the door released an agonized wail and fell back toward the cabin. Although he knew he had hit the shooter, Burton was unable to tell where his bullets had struck in the darkness. He leaned around to get a glance at the prone figure on the ground.

'Rot in hell, Burton!' screamed a voice from the darkness of the cabin.

A pistol roared from just within the doorway and Burton fell backward. A bullet whizzed past him and he realized it was Emerson Dodge inside the cabin. He reached out and took Maynard Blayloch's arm, then dragged the unmoving man back with him behind the woodpile. In the moonlight he could see blood seeping from a wound in the deputy's chest. Blayloch was seriously wounded but still breathing.

Burton heard movement on the other side of the woodpile. He saw the dark outlines of two men running across the short strip of yard to the barn. One was helping the other stay on his feet. Burton raised his pistol and considered shooting at them, but he couldn't bring himself to shoot a man in the back — not even someone like Emerson Dodge.

He looked down at Blayloch, who was still unconscious. He heard sounds from within the barn and fixed his eyes across the yard. Moments later, he watched two horsemen bolt from the barn and ride away across the pasture toward the distant mountains. He could only barely discern them in the darkness, but he noticed that the rider closest to him was slumping over in the saddle.

A drizzling rain began to pour. Burton knelt and put his arms around Blayloch's torso, taking care not to touch his wound. He lifted the man's upper body and pulled him around the woodpile and through the back door into the kitchen of Dodge's cabin. The rain was coming down hard by the time he laid him on the floor.

Burton felt gently around the wound through the hole in Blayloch's sheepskin coat. The blood seemed to have congealed to a certain extent. Perhaps the injury wasn't as bad as it had first appeared, Burton thought. He leaned close to Blayloch's left ear and spoke.

'Maynard, can you hear me?' he asked in a loud voice. 'It's Ed Burton. Can you hear what I'm saying?' There was no response; the only sound was the raindrops hitting the cabin. They made dull thumping noises against the windows.

Burton felt around on a shelf above the stove and found a lantern, which he lighted and placed on the table. He considered his options, quickly realizing they were limited. Emerson Dodge and his companion were both armed and dangerous, despite the latter's wounds. They had ridden off toward the rugged and, in some places, impassable mountains to the south. Burton had never been in those mountains, unlike Dodge and, he remembered, Blayloch.

Solitary pursuit was out of the question. He needed to get help for Blayloch and round up a posse to pursue the men in the mountains. Blayloch's condition appeared to have stabilized, at least for the time being. His eyes were still closed, but his breathing was even and less shallow than it had been. Had Burton not seen the deputy's wound, he would almost believe the man was sleeping peacefully rather than grievously injured.

He would be safe here while Burton rode into Oakridge and summoned the doctor. There was no way Dodge and his companion would return to Deception Creek after what had just happened.

★   ★   ★

Burton rode into Oakridge twenty minutes later. By this time, dawn was creeping across the sky. Burton rode directly to the home of the town's only physician, whom he roused. It wasn't long before the doctor was on the road toward Deception Creek and Emerson Dodge's cabin, accompanied by his teenage son and a shotgun. Burton assured them that the gun wouldn't be necessary, but he understood their desire to carry protection. Whether Emerson Dodge was the Phantom or not, he was clearly a dangerous and violent man, with no compunction about shooting at lawmen with the intent to kill.

Burton rode to the telegrapher's

office down the street from the doctor's home. It was owned and operated by an old man who slept on a cot at the back of the building. Burton woke him and had him send a telegram to Eugene, informing the sheriff there of the situation and of Burton's intent to form a posse and pursue Dodge.

The first person Burton considered for the posse was Hank Kirby. The man was tough, knew his way around a gun, and had seen the work of the Phantom first hand. He was respected by everyone in the community. Burton rode from the telegraph office to the Kirby property just outside Oakridge. He wasn't surprised to find Hank Kirby awake already, sipping coffee and smoking a cigar in a chair on his front porch.

Kirby rose when he spotted Burton emerge from the trees.

'Morning, Mr Burton,' he said with what Burton considered excessive deference. 'What can I do for you?'

'All hell just broke loose out at Emerson Dodge's place,' Burton explained, halting his horse near Kirby's porch. 'Maynard's been shot. The doc's on his way out there to fetch him. He's still alive and he's not bleeding too bad.'

'By God,' Kirby said. He set his cup down on the railing of the porch and shook his head. 'Where's Dodge?'

'He and some other sidewinder blasted their way out of Deception Creek. They headed for the mountains just south of the property. You ever been there?'

Kirby's eyes narrowed and he nodded thoughtfully. 'I've been there. That's not a place you want to head into if you don't know your way around.'

'That's what I was thinking, too,' Burton said. 'I'm putting a posse together right now.'

Kirby raised a hand. 'Give me a minute or two and I'll be ready to ride with you.'

'I am much obliged,' Burton said with a tired grin. The bottoms of his feet were hurting badly and he was exhausted. He looked up to see Ethel Kirby, Hank's kindly and soft-spoken wife, walk out of the cabin door carrying a cup of coffee. She reached out and offered it to Burton.

'Thought you might be able to use this,' she said.

He accepted it with gratitude.

'Thank you, ma'am,' he said. 'Boy, do I need it!'

She smiled and turned back into the house. Burton sat quietly for a few minutes, sipping his coffee and trying to ignore the pain in his feet. The beverage had its intended effect very quickly.

He was surer than ever that the Phantom was Emerson Dodge. Why else had Dodge chosen gunfire rather than talk to him and Blayloch? Dodge's time in the Oakridge area happened to coincide precisely with last year's Phantom attacks as well as those from five years before.

Hank Kirby came out on the porch, buttoning his coat with one hand while he placed his hat firmly on his head with the other.

'I'm going to get my horse and we'll

be on our way,' he said.

Burton nodded and finished the last few gulps of his coffee.

Ten minutes later they rode into Oakridge. Burton was surprised to find three men waiting for them in front of Maynard Blayloch's office. The largest of them, a huge redheaded fellow named Otis Thompson, waved at Burton and Kirby, although his face was somber.

'Morning, Mr Kirby,' Thompson said, then looked at Burton. 'Mr Burton.'

'Morning, gentlemen,' Burton replied.

'We're ready to join your posse,' Thompson explained. 'My brother and I passed Doctor Rodgers when he was going out to Deception Creek. He told us what happened to Maynard. We got Tim Beach with us' — he gestured toward the short blond-haired man behind him — 'and Frank O'Rourke will be here in a few minutes. He's bringing provisions in case we're in the mountains for a couple days.'

Burton was astonished; he had never had a posse materialize without having organized it himself.

'Mr Burton is in charge here,' Hank Kirby said.

The three men nodded without hesitation. Otis Thompson met Burton's eyes.

'Cindy Ballard was my cousin,' he said, anger in his face. Burton realized then that more than just two people in Oakridge suspected Emerson Dodge of being the Phantom.

'Any of you men familiar with the mountains just south of the Dodge place?' he queried.

The Thompson brothers, who were practically twins, shook their heads. Tim Beach nodded.

'Been there once, back when I was a kid. They got caves in those mountains, you know. He might be hiding in one of them.'

Burton remembered Maynard Blayloch's comment about the caves in the mountains. 'Do you know where the caves are?' he asked.

'No,' Beach said. 'It's been a long

time since I been there.'

'I do,' Kirby interjected. 'I know exactly where they are.'

'Good,' Burton said. He spotted a man riding toward them from the west end of town. The rider's saddlebags bulged.

'There's Frank,' said Otis Thompson.

Otis' brother hadn't said a word, but Burton thought he looked agreeable enough, and tough as well. He remembered the man's name was Martin.

O'Rourke pulled reins a few feet away and nodded in greeting.

'Ready when y'all are,' he said. 'Morning, Hank. Morning, Mr Burton.'

'Good morning, Frank,' Burton said.

O'Rourke patted one of his saddlebags. 'I got enough food in here to last us three or four days,' he said.

'I reckon that'll cover it,' Burton said. 'Appreciate your help, men. Now let's head out.'

8

They ran into Doctor Rodgers and his son about a mile west of Oakridge. The posse moved over to the side of the road to make way for the wagon. Doctor Rodgers halted the wagon and Burton looked over the side at Maynard Blayloch. The deputy was covered with several blankets. He looked deathly pale and was sweating heavily as he opened his eyes and looked at Burton.

'Maynard, you're awake!' Burton said.

Blayloch attempted a smile. 'Good to see you, Mr Burton.'

'We got the posse together. You go back to town and we'll see you again soon. Don't worry — we'll get him.'

Blayloch lifted his head and looked at the men who were riding with Burton.

'Sure wish I was going with you,' he said plaintively.

'Can't be helped,' Burton said. 'Let the doc take care of you. We're going to hit the trail.' He waved at the physician and led the posse away from the wagon toward Deception Creek.

It was nearly full daylight when they rode into Emerson Dodge's yard. Although Burton had intended to proceed directly to the mountains, he felt compelled to stop for a moment when he saw that the back door had been left open. They halted between the barn and the cabin and Burton dismounted.

'I want to take a look in the house,' he said. He handed his reins to Hank Kirby. 'Be right out.'

He walked to the back door, trying not to let the men see the pain he was experiencing from his feet. The lantern was still burning brightly in the kitchen when Burton stepped into the house. Now that he had a moment to look around, he found that the place was filthy, with a musty odor in the air.

Unwashed dishes were piled on the

table. He saw some blood on the dirt floor that must have soaked through Maynard Blayloch's coat. There was nothing else of interest in the kitchen. Burton proceeded into the short hallway and looked into the cabin's sole bedroom. He stopped short and drew a sharp breath.

'Lord Almighty,' he said quietly.

Beside a small, dingy looking bed was a wooden chair. On the seat of the chair was a burlap mask. Burton entered the room and picked up the mask. He noticed the eye holes — and he remembered those predatory eyes that had seemed to be staring at him from the trees outside his house. Now he knew whose eyes those had been. Emerson Dodge was the Phantom. He must have been so scared when Burton and Blayloch showed up at his cabin that he forgot to take his mask with him when he fled.

Burton retraced his steps through the house and exited out of the back door. He closed it behind him and moved toward his horse, trying in vain to walk in a manner that wouldn't send shooting pains through his feet. He took his reins from Hank Kirby and held up the mask. All the men looked at it.

'This is the Phantom's mask,' Burton announced. He looked at each of the men in turn. 'I just found it in the bedroom here. Emerson Dodge is the Phantom.' He lowered the mask and examined it for a moment. 'He tried to kill me and my wife last night. That's why Maynard and I came out here.' He put the mask in his left saddle-bag and mounted. Without another word, he touched spurs and led the men across the pasture toward the mountains.

* * *

It took a little over an hour for the posse to reach the mountains. A merciless rain started to drench them soon after they left Emerson Dodge's cabin. They removed their slickers from their saddle-bags and pulled their hats down low on their heads.

A trail snaked up through the trees and disappeared from view around the side of a mountain. The men could see fresh hoof prints in the thick mud ahead of them. They halted at the beginning of the trail and Burton turned to Hank Kirby.

'Hank, you know your way around here. How about you lead the way?'

Kirby spurred his horse up to the front of the group and pulled reins beside Burton. His eyes followed the tracks up to where they vanished in the trees on the mountainside.

'We're going to have to be real careful when we get in there,' he said. 'The trail leads into a gully after about a quarter mile. They could be on either side of it, ready to ambush us, once we get in there. We'll have to keep a good eye out.'

Kirby spurred his horse gently and the animal began to move up the trail. Burton was just behind Kirby, followed by the Thompson brothers, Tim Beach, and Frank O'Rourke, all of whom had removed their rifles from their scabbards and laid them across their thighs in the event of an ambush.

The rain continued to assault them as they left the level ground behind. The trail skirted the side of the small mountain, then turned south into a wide valley between two larger peaks. The men paused at the top of the trail before following it into the valley. From where they sat in their saddles they had a good view of the terrain below them.

Burton removed his field glasses from a saddle-bag. The possibility of an ambush was distinct, but only if the two fugitives had decided not to make a run for it. If they were lying in wait somewhere up ahead in the trees, then Burton figured it must be because the injured partner was unable to travel any further.

He scanned the tree-lined ridges up ahead, searching patiently for any sign of movement or perhaps the glint of sunlight on a rifle barrel. He found nothing after examining the valley for a few minutes.

'All right, let's get a move on,' he said finally. 'Keep those rifles handy.'

Burton heeled his horse forward, this time taking the lead instead of Hank Kirby. As the leader of the posse, he wanted the men to know he would take all the risks with them. They moved down the narrow trail in a line, maintaining a slow but steady pace. Burton cursed the fog that had settled in the trees and seeped down into the gully. The rain, at least, had diminished, but there was still a persistent drizzle.

Trees lined both sides of the trail. Burton could still see the tracks left by the fleeing pair. It took the posse nearly an hour to traverse the gully, and their vulnerability to attack made the tension high amongst the men. Burton was relieved when the trail began to twist up and around the side of another mountain, taking them out of the gully.

He slowed down and let Hank Kirby come up alongside him as the posse began the ascent up the mountain trail.

'They're hoping to outrun us,' Burton

commented. 'I don't think they'll try an ambush now. They would have had good cover back in that gully. They could have blasted us from both sides.'

Kirby shifted in the saddle, his lean face reflecting a grim determination.

'We'll reach the caves in about an hour, maybe an hour and a half.'

'Good,' Burton said.

'Do they have much in the way of provisions?' Kirby asked.

Burton adjusted his spectacles.

'I don't think so,' he said. 'They shot their way out of that cabin and lit out from the barn in a hurry. I don't think they'd packed their saddle-bags before they ran for it. They weren't expecting me and Maynard to show up.'

'Well, they can run as hard as they want, but if they don't have food, there's no way they'll make it out of these mountains. If they try to shoot a deer in here, we'll hear their position. They may just have to surrender.'

Burton shook his head. 'That'd be a convenient turn of events, but those boys are desperate. They were out for blood last night.'

'I wonder if that other feller with Emerson ain't his brother.'

'I wondered that myself. You know his brother?'

'Not really. His name is Dalton. He'd sometimes come visit Buck Dodge along with Emerson and their pa. I think he lives up in Salem.'

'Yes, that's what we'd heard. Emerson Dodge hasn't been seen around town for over a week. Maynard heard he was up visiting his brother.'

'A shame things turned out this way. Their uncle wasn't a bad man. Neither was their pa.'

'You never know what people are capable of. I wonder how Dalton Dodge is mixed up in the Phantom case, if he is.'

'They ever have two attackers when the Phantom struck?'

'Not that I know of,' Burton replied. 'Whatever his involvement with the Phantom is, he was more than willing to come out shooting with his brother. I don't know how Maynard isn't dead. I thought he was a goner for sure when I first saw him go down.'

Kirby was silent for a minute, then said, 'You said the Phantom tried to get into your place?'

'Yep. He was lurking in the trees across the yard from the front room. If I hadn't been stoking the fire, I wouldn't have seen him. I was able to wake up Annie and get guns in both our hands without him knowing.' Burton adjusted his hat against the rain. 'He was coming in through the back door and I took him by surprise. He outran me and must've got back to his horse. That gave him plenty of time to get back to the Dodge place.'

The trail had leveled off, and soon began another short descent into a canyon that was thick with timber. The forested mountainsides loomed above the posse on both sides. Kirby signaled to Burton.

'First of the caves is up here on the

right a little ways ahead,' he said.

Burton looked in the direction the homesteader had indicated. The fog was thinner there, he observed with some relief. On the far end of a ridge he saw the opening to a large hole in the side of the mountain, partially obscured by the trees around it. There was no sign of life near the opening of the cave.

'The way that cave is situated we should be able to approach it without being shot at,' Kirby added. 'I'd be surprised if they was hiding out in that one, though, because there are more caves a few miles down the trail that would give them better cover if they're expecting to trade fire with us.'

'We'll have to check it out anyway,' Burton said.

'That's what I figured,' Kirby said with a nod.

Burton brought the posse to a halt. The men congregated around him, waiting for instructions. Although they had been riding for nearly five hours by now, none of them looked tired. This pleased Burton, who knew they likely had many more hours of riding ahead of them.

'We're coming up on the first cave,' he said. 'Hank, how do you suggest we make our approach?'

Kirby sat back in the saddle and looked at the trees on the incline leading up to the cave.

'If we send a few men up from the side here, the others can cover them from a little further down the trail.' He pointed to the cave and the heads of all the posse members turned to look with him. 'If someone's in the cave and tries to get a shot off at us, they'd be exposed to gunfire. That's why I said I don't think they'll choose to hide in this one — the Dodge boys know this terrain and they know which caves will work in a shootout and which won't. We have to make sure, though.'

Burton chose Kirby and the Thompson brothers to make the approach up the incline. They waited while Burton, Tim Beach, and Frank O'Rourke moved into position to give them cover.

Beach and O'Rourke rode past Burton. All three men dismounted and moved into the trees below the cave. Rifles in hand, they each had an unobstructed view of the cave opening. Burton was closest to Kirby and the Thompsons. He signaled to Kirby to proceed.

The men by the trail watched as their three fellow posse members picketed their horses in the trees and began to climb the incline to the mouth of the cave. O'Rourke had his Winchester fixed on the entrance, while Beach and Burton stood by alertly, their rifles at the ready.

Kirby and the Thompson brothers reached the rock wall to the right of the cave. All three had their pistols in their hands, ready for the worst. They crept closer to the edge of the entrance and paused, listening intently. Apart from the steady but light rain and the wind moving through the trees, there was only silence for several seconds.

Then Kirby stiffened and held up a

hand. He had heard something from inside the cave. Burton's eyes moved to Otis and Martin Thompson. Their faces were tense. Burton knew they had heard something in the cave, too.

Kirby communicated something to the brothers with his eyes and the Thompsons nodded. After another brief pause, Kirby suddenly pivoted around to the opening of the cave and dropped down into a crouching position, his pistol extended toward the shadows. Burton was prepared to hear gunfire. He looked to the other men on the trail with him and realized that they, too, were expecting a shootout.

Had the Dodge brothers really taken refuge in the one cave that, according to Hank Kirby, offered them the least protection in the event of an attack? Burton watched the crouching form of Hank Kirby. After a moment, Kirby rose, muttered something to the Thompson brothers, and then stepped into the cave.

'What in the hell?' Burton asked quietly.

Seconds later, Kirby emerged, leading a horse by its reins. He called down to Burton: 'I think you better come up here. I found Dalton Dodge.'

Burton looked at O'Rourke and Beach. 'You men stay in position.'

'Yes, sir,' said Beach. O'Rourke nodded, his rifle still gripped firmly in his hands although no longer pointed toward the cave. His eyes were scanning the ridges further along the trail.

Burton climbed up the incline through the trees. When he reached the ledge, he approached Kirby and looked into the cave. Although there was only a little illumination inside from the limited sunlight, he could see well enough. Inside he espied a young man whom he didn't recognize lying on the floor of the cave. The man's head rested on a roll of blankets, and another blanket covered his body. A pistol lay on the ground not far from his hand, but he made no attempt to reach for it. His eyes were closed and he almost appeared to be dead, with skin so pale it seemed as if all the blood had been drained from his body. But Burton could see that the man's chest was moving ever so slightly. He was alive — at least for now.

'That's Dalton Dodge,' said Kirby. He handed the reins of the horse off to Martin Thompson, who led the animal down to the trees and picketed it there.

Burton leaned his rifle against the wall of the cave. He pulled his Navy Colt from its holster and walked over to where Dalton Dodge lay. He leaned over quickly and picked up the man's pistol from the blanket. He put it in his waistband and slipped his own gun back into the holster, then nudged Dodge with the toe of his boot.

'Dodge,' he said, loudly and firmly. He nudged him again. 'Dalton Dodge!'

The wounded man coughed hideously and opened his eyes, which took in both Burton and Kirby without seeming to focus. He coughed again. Sweat had broken out on his forehead.

'You Dalton Dodge?' Burton asked.

The man on the ground flicked his

eyes up to Burton's face.

'Yeah,' he said. 'That's my name.'

'You're under arrest for attempting to murder the deputy sheriff of Oakridge,' Burton informed him. 'Where's your brother?'

'How the hell would I know?' Dodge asked. 'If you look hard enough, maybe you'll find him.'

Burton leaned over and ripped the blanket off him. Blood from two bullet wounds had seeped through his shirt and was beginning to puddle on the ground beside him.

'You're going to die soon,' said Burton, with no trace of pity in his voice. 'If you want your brother to have a fair trial for his crimes, then you need to tell us what we want to know.'

Dodge blinked and a disdainful smirk formed on his lips. 'Hell, I don't care what you do with Emerson,' he said. 'He left me here.' He glanced at Kirby. 'His own brother! Can you believe that?'

He laughed bitterly. Burton suspected that, had the situation been reversed, Dalton would have done the same thing to Emerson. He had tangled with a lot of bad men in his life, and he knew a killer when he saw one. Dalton Dodge was a killer, Burton thought. Just like his brother.

'Is he coming back?' Burton asked.

'Highly doubtful,' sneered Dodge. 'Let's put it that way.' He had possessed an innate dislike for lawmen his entire life, and finding himself perched on the threshold of death only intensified that sentiment.

'Fair enough,' Burton concluded. He clearly wasn't going to acquire any useful information from the dying man. He turned to Kirby. 'Get the rest of the men ready. We'll head out presently.'

Kirby nodded and exited the cave.

Burton took a deep breath and looked back at Dalton Dodge.

'We're going to catch your brother,' he said flatly. 'If you're still alive when we come back this way then we'll take you to Oakridge and you can stand trial.' He shot a sharp glance at the blood stains on Dodge's shirt. 'I don't think you'll be around for that, though.' He turned back to the cave entrance.

'Hey!' screamed the man on the ground. 'You can't leave me like this! I'm entitled to a fair trial! I'll bleed to death in here!'

Burton looked at Dodge with a thin smile. 'I suspect that's a more peaceful death than you deserve,' he said, then turned and walked out of the cave. He heard Dalton Dodge yelling for help as he descended the incline and mounted his horse.

'Emerson Dodge left his brother behind,' he told the posse. 'He's got quite a head start, so we're going to have to ride hard.'

He touched spurs to his horse's flanks and started back down the trail, the other men following closely behind.

* * *

Apart from hoof tracks that disappeared as the mud gave way to rockier ground, the posse saw no sign of Emerson Dodge for the rest of the day. They checked the caves further down the valley, approaching cautiously in each case, but he was nowhere to be found.

'He's trying to make his way south, out of the mountains,' Burton ventured.

Hank Kirby agreed. 'If he was going to try to hold us off, the caves would have been the best place to do it. Without food, though, he won't get far.'

Burton called a halt to the pursuit not long after dusk. The men and their animals were fatigued. They had had only a quick meal of jerky and hard tack in the saddle since that morning. They moved into the brush off the side of the trail and made camp for the night beneath a ledge of rock. O'Rourke got a fire going and, removing a bag of coffee from his saddle-bag, started boiling water. After the coffee was ready, he got out a skillet and began cooking bacon and beans.

In the firelight, Burton looked around at the faces of the other men. He was grateful that the overhanging outcropping of rock sheltered them from the rain. The smell of hot food was already raising his spirits, and he knew it would raise the spirits of the rest of the posse, too.

O'Rourke distributed tin cups among the men and poured the coffee. It was hot and bitter, but Burton didn't mind. He watched the men as they removed their horses' saddles and brushed the animals down.

Tim Beach was standing nearby, fashioning a cigarette. He licked it and poked it between his lips, then snapped a match alight with his thumb, held it to the cigarette, and inhaled deeply. Smoke slithered out of his nostrils as he stared into the fire.

'I can take first watch tonight, Mr Burton,' he said. 'I always have a hard time falling asleep at night as it is.'

'That works for me,' Burton confirmed.

After a few minutes, O'Rourke removed tin plates and forks from a bulging saddle-bag. He had made a lot of food and doled out generous portions to the men, who accepted their plates eagerly. Several minutes passed without anyone uttering a word.

O'Rourke finished his meal and reached into his jacket, from which he removed a flask.

'Anyone in the mood for some libations?' he asked.

With the exception of Burton and Kirby, the men partook, and did so enthusiastically. Because the flask wasn't very large, Burton wasn't worried about the men imbibing to excess. They passed it around, some pouring the whiskey into their coffee, some taking a slug directly from the flask. The alcohol lifted the collective mood nearly as much as the food had.

Maybe more, Burton thought with a quiet chuckle. He decided to divide up the watches now so that the men could go to sleep as soon as possible. They would all be rising early in the morning and Burton had no doubt that tomor-row would be a long day, whether they caught up with Emerson Dodge or not.

'We'll do two-hour watches tonight,' he announced.

The men followed his words carefully.

'Tim Beach here has volunteered to take the first watch. Anyone want to volunteer for the second?'

Otis Thompson held up his hand and Burton nodded in acknowledgement.

'How about the third watch?'

Martin Thompson put his hand up at the same time as O'Rourke. Burton chose Thompson to relieve his brother.

'I'll take the first watch tomorrow night,' said Burton. 'Hank and Frank can take the other two. I encourage y'all to get to sleep as soon you can. We're going to need it.'

There was no argument from the tired horsemen. They untied their bed rolls from behind their saddles and soon were sleeping deeply in various places around the fire. Beach periodically checked the fire, which he maintained at a low burn. He spent the rest of his watch perched atop a nearby boulder that afforded him an expansive view of the surrounding area. Anyone who attempted to sneak up on the sleeping posse would be spotted.

A little over two hours later, Beach awakened Otis Thompson, who took his place on the boulder. The rain began to fall steadily shortly after Thompson assumed the watch. He walked back to the camp and put his slicker on. Nothing stirred in the shadowy mountain forests around him. This isolated area had only rarely been traversed by humans.

Martin Thompson was already wide awake when his brother went to shake him. He assumed the watch and kept a keen eye out until dawn spread its varied hues across the sky. It wasn't long before O'Rourke rolled out of his blankets and began boiling coffee. The aroma roused the other men and they quickly got out of their bedrolls and stood around the fire. Soon they were drinking coffee again.

Martin Thompson climbed down off the boulder and rejoined the rest of the posse. He accepted a tin cup filled with coffee and took a large gulp from it, seemingly oblivious to the liquid's scalding heat.

They broke camp shortly thereafter and continued up the trail. They soon found Dodge's tracks as the ground became muddy; in his haste to outrun the posse he had made no attempt to hide his trail. For Burton, this only confirmed Kirby's earlier observation that Dodge's plan now was to escape through the mountains to the south.

'Hank, how easy will it be for him to get through those mountains south of here?' Burton asked.

Kirby's face indicated that Dodge's task was all but impossible.

'From here to the southern edge of the range, there's nothing but dead-end gullies and mountain passes that lead nowhere. He might have more familiarity with these mountains than most of the people in Oakridge, but I doubt he's spent much time all the way down here. He and his pa used to stay in those caves and use that as a base for their hunting. They didn't come all the way out here. He very well could get lost if he's not careful, particularly since he's not prepared for an extended stay in the wilderness. If he strays from the trail here and makes one wrong turn up in the mountains, he might never find his way out.'

Burton wouldn't have lost any sleep at the thought of Dodge getting lost in the hills and dying a lonely death, but he desperately wanted to capture the man alive and take him back to Oakridge for trial.

These were his thoughts as he led the posse down a small rise and around a cluster of trees. Suddenly he yanked his horse's reins and brought the animal to a halt. The other men followed suit almost instantly. Kirby heeled his horse forward and came up beside Burton.

'What is it, Mr Burton?' he asked.

Burton raised a hand and pointed

down to the edge of the timber, roughly fifty yards from where his men sat in their saddles. Kirby's face tightened when he saw what Burton had indicated.

Standing on a small grassy embankment between the trail and the rim of the trees was Emerson Dodge's horse.

9

Burton turned and waved the men off the trail into the trees. They moved several yards into the firs and dismounted, holding their horses by the reins.

'Dodge's horse is just up ahead,' said Burton quietly as he stepped down from the saddle.

'Is he on it?' asked Beach.

Burton shook his head. 'You men stand by here,' he said. 'Hank, come with me.'

Burton and Kirby drew their weapons and moved cautiously through the trees until they were able to see Dodge's horse again. It hadn't moved, and was munching the wet grass on the embankment.

The men watched the horse for a few minutes. Only when it took a stumbling step forward toward the trees did they see why it had been left alone on the trail. It was holding its front left leg at an awkward, unnatural angle, and its limp when it attempted to walk was painful to watch. The horse had hurt itself, and badly. That much was evident to both Burton and Kirby.

'He rode it hard, that's for sure,' Kirby said. 'Someone needs to put it out of its misery.'

'He didn't want to give away his position with a gunshot,' Burton suggested. 'Either that, or he doesn't care if his horse suffers.'

'Probably both,' Kirby said.

Burton's eyes scanned the trees up ahead near where the horse was standing. He saw no sign of Emerson Dodge. He looked across the trail into the trees on the left, but again he saw nothing.

'He might be hiding in the forest somewhere down the trail,' he said. 'I don't think he's around here. He wants to stay on the move.' He looked toward Dodge's horse. 'I'm going to take care of that.'

He moved quickly out of the trees and walked toward the horse until he was five feet from it. The animal was too tired and in too much pain to try to run from Burton. It was standing still, its lame leg held aloft, when Burton removed his Navy Colt from its holster and fired one shot through its right eye. The sound of the shot reverberated through the trees and up the side of the surrounding mountains. The animal fell dead where it stood.

Burton walked back to where the men were standing and divided the posse in two, sending the Thompson brothers and O'Rourke into the trees across the trail. They were to spread out and move to the south, searching for Dodge in the forest, while Burton, Kirby, and Beach searched the east side of the trail. Burton stayed close to the edge of the trees, while Kirby moved into the forest about fifty yards to Burton's right. Beach moved a few dozen yards to the right of Kirby. They moved forward at a slow but steady pace, leading their horses by the reins as they did so.

The posse had advanced several hundred feet when O'Rourke called for them to halt. They stopped in place, silently watching him approach a downed tree. There was ample room for someone to hide behind it. Martin Thompson moved forward and took cover behind a large maple; from where he stood, he could cover O'Rourke. O'Rourke hesitated for a moment and then sprang from behind the gnarled roots, his pistol extended. He found nothing and signaled to Thompson. The posse resumed their dogged southward tracking.

They had gone about a mile when a shot rang out. The men froze at first, confused about the direction from which the shot had come, then quickly dropped their horses' reins and took cover. The horses darted away through the woods, the sound of the shot echoing behind them for several seconds.

'That's far enough!' a voice bellowed.

Burton instantly recognized it as that of Emerson Dodge. It came from somewhere in the trees, up ahead to the right.

'I have all of you sons of bitches covered! Don't try anything funny.'

Burton's pulse pounded in his ears. Dodge was making his last stand; he wouldn't ever be more dangerous than he was at this moment. Burton had hoped they might be able to take him by surprise, but that was out of the question now.

So be it, Burton thought. He examined his surroundings and concluded that Dodge was probably lying about having the entire posse covered from his vantage point. They were spread out too far in the trees on both sides of the trail for Dodge to have them all pinned down.

He looked toward Hank Kirby, who had taken cover behind a giant fir tree over to Burton's right and was hidden from view. Burton looked across the trail and had a clear view of Otis

Thompson sitting with his back against a tree, his rifle resting in the crook of his arm.

Thompson was looking over his left shoulder up toward the trees on the mountainside whence he had heard Dodge's voice.

Thompson's gaze shifted and met Burton's. He squinted and jerked his head in the direction where he had been looking a moment before.

Burton twisted and glanced up through the branches at the mountain that loomed over his side of the trail. Then he looked back toward Thompson, who nodded confidently and raised his rifle, holding it in front of him for a few seconds before pivoting and rolling through the undergrowth to the cover of another nearby tree. Suddenly he raised the rifle and pressed it firmly against his right shoulder. He squeezed his left eye closed, took a quick aim, and fired. He quickly levered another shot and fired, then twice more in quick succession.

Immediately after the last shot the men heard an anguished shriek from up in the trees, right where Thompson had directed his fire.

Burton waited a few moments, then yelled: 'Dodge! You have no chance of escape. Give up now before we have to kill you.'

'I'll kill at least half of you before you lay hands on me!' Dodge shouted back.

'You've already been shot!' Burton called.

Dodge's retort was contemptuous. 'You think I'm scared of dying?'

'We know you ain't scared of killing. That's why you got a posse after you.' Burton paused, thinking. 'You're going back whether you like it or not. Dead or alive — which is it going to be?'

'I guess we're going to find out, ain't we?'

Clouds gathered above the posse and, within minutes, a steady rain began to pour. Burton decided to wait until nightfall before making a move. He couldn't take the chance of a daylight attack that could very well end with Dodge killing two or three of the posse, if not more.

He would have the men approach Dodge's position from the north and the south simultaneously. He surmised that Dodge had been seriously injured by Otis Thompson's bullet. Once darkness robbed him of his tactical advantage, Dodge would be fairly easy to capture. If he wanted to go out in a blaze of glory rather than stand trial for his crimes, then that was his decision.

Hank Kirby had been able to shift his position slightly and now had an unobstructed view of Burton. Through a combination of hand signals and mouthing words without speaking, Burton was able to communicate his plan to the rancher. He turned to Otis Thompson and explained the plan to him in the same manner. Both Kirby and Thompson indicated their understanding.

Finally, the only thing left to do was wait until sundown.

* * *

For the first time since the posse had left Oakridge, Burton was happy to see a heavy fog move down from the mountains. The fog oozed through the trees in which the men were hiding and spread across the trail itself.

Four hours passed before darkness fell. Dodge shouted occasional threats, but apart from that the woods were quiet. The men tried to make themselves as comfortable as possible while biding their time.

Although he couldn't be entirely sure, Burton thought that Dodge had moved a little further up in the timber after being shot by Otis Thompson. He wondered where the fugitive had been hit and how badly he was bleeding.

Night had fallen when Burton gave the signal — one piercingly loud whistle. He gripped his rifle and moved in a crouching position toward where he had last seen Kirby. He reached him quickly, concealed from above by the fog. Tim Beach emerged from the trees on their right a few seconds later. Kirby and Beach moved close to Burton, whose whisper was barely audible.

'We're going to go up in the trees there and move in on Dodge from the north. The other three are going to go south a ways and cross the trail. They'll approach him from there.' He directed his next words to Hank Kirby. 'You stay here. His only chance to escape is to try to come down through the trees here. If he does, you be waiting.'

Burton tapped Beach on the shoulder and they moved away from the trailside toward the base of the mountain. The fog seemed to get thicker as the sky grew darker. Their rifles in hand, the two men moved quietly up the incline.

The trees were close together, hindering their movement. Within fifteen minutes they were in a position that Burton thought was roughly parallel to where he had last heard Dodge's voice. With Beach at his side, Burton paused and knelt between two trees. They were waiting to allow the posse members further south to get into position.

Presently, Burton rose. Beach followed him as he picked his way south on the mountainside, taking his time and scanning the trees ahead of him. The fog was thinner here, which made their job easier.

Moving around an especially bulky tree, Burton abruptly stopped. He raised a hand, halting Beach, who craned his neck and looked over Burton's shoulder. He saw it, too, then — a dark human shape stretched out on a bedroll in a patch of bare ground beneath the trees. The form was unmoving and gave no indication that it had heard their approach.

The two men waited, Burton's eyes searching the trees across the clearing. Only a minute passed before he saw the shadowy forms of the Thompson brothers and Frank O'Rourke looming there. They observed Emerson Dodge on his bedroll. Burton made a few hand gestures to them, and then all five left the cover of the trees and moved toward the man on the ground.

They were ten feet away from him on either side when Dodge opened his eyes and sat upright, simultaneously pulling a pistol from his holster. He turned to his left, raised the gun, and fired. Tim Beach yelled in shock and pain, then tumbled face-first on to the ground. Dodge swung his pistol around to his right to fire at O'Rourke and the Thompsons, but Burton leapt forward and slammed the butt of his rifle into Dodge's head, which snapped backward. The fugitive fell back on his bedroll and lay there unconscious.

'His neck might be broken,' Martin Thompson said.

Burton and O'Rourke walked quickly to the prone figure of Tim Beach. Burton rolled him over and saw the bullet wound in the left side of his chest.

'Went straight through his heart,' O'Rourke observed mournfully. 'Damn it.'

Burton felt sick for a moment. Emerson Dodge had killed his last victim. It would be one more crime for which he would hang.

The Thompsons tied Dodge's wrists behind his back. They pointed out the bullet wound to the groin that Otis Thompson had given him. O'Rourke knelt beside Dodge and smacked the man's face a few times.

'Dodge!' he said. 'Dodge — wake up!'

He opened his canteen and poured water on Dodge's face, then smacked him again. Dodge's eyes slowly opened, and the Thompsons dragged him roughly to his feet. O'Rourke, a large, strong man, put Beach's body over his shoulder. They followed Burton and descended slowly down the mountainside. The Thompson brothers had to hold Dodge by the arms to keep him vertical. He mumbled incoherent threats that were ignored by the posse. Burton's blow to the head seemed to have left him without the full use of his faculties, at least temporarily.

They met Hank Kirby in the trees between the base of the mountain and the trail.

'By God,' Kirby said softly. 'The son of a bitch got Tim.'

He shook his head sadly. It was the first time Burton had heard Kirby use language like that.

★   ★   ★

It was nearly dusk on the second day of travelling back to Oakridge when they reached the cave where they had found Dalton Dodge. Burton and Kirby left their horses on the trail with the men and climbed up through the firs to the mouth of the cave.

Burton saw it first, and a wave of nausea came over him as he turned away. Kirby stepped beside him and took in the scene with a penetrating glance. He drew a deep breath. He and Burton exchanged a look and began moving back down toward the waiting posse.

'He in there?' asked O'Rourke with concern in his voice.

Burton put a foot in a stirrup and pivoted up into his saddle.

'Some of him's in there,' he said grimly. 'Black bear must have got him.' He picked up his reins, his face somber. 'He might have already been dead when the bear found him. He was bleeding pretty good when we left him.'

His hands tied securely to his saddlehorn, Emerson Dodge said nothing.

10

It was just after nine o'clock in the morning when the posse rode into Oakridge.

They drew leather at the hitching post in front of Maynard Blayloch's office. Kirby volunteered to take the body out to the Beach place and inform the man's wife and children that he had been killed. Burton thanked Kirby for taking on such an unpleasant task, and for his help during the hunt for the Dodge brothers. Kirby nodded, obviously uncomfortable with Burton's praise.

'If you need me again, Mr Burton, you know where to find me,' he said. He turned his horse toward the west end of the street and slowly rode off, leading Beach's horse by the reins.

Burton dismounted and realized he didn't have a key to Blayloch's office door. The jail was located at the back of the building, behind the deputy's office.

As if he were reading Burton's mind, O'Rourke said, 'Mr Burton, I'll ride over to the doctor's and get the key from Maynard.' His eyes regarded Dodge with distaste.

'Then we can get this trash locked up.'

Dodge turned his head and glared at O'Rourke. As he had done for virtually the entire trip back from the mountains, he chose to say nothing. His face expressed both hatred and exhaustion.

'That'll be fine, Frank,' Burton said. 'Thank you.'

O'Rourke rode away, returning a few minutes later with the key. Burton and the Thompson brothers were standing under the awning in front of the office; they had left Dodge sitting on his horse. Burton took the key and opened the door as the brothers removed Dodge from his mount and pushed him into the office.

'Welcome home, Dodge,' said Burton as he unlocked the door to the cells.

'This will be where you spend the last days of your miserable life.'

Dodge's lips curled contemptuously. 'I still get a trial, Burton.'

'True,' Burton responded. 'But four people watched you kill Tim Beach. You won't get around that in a court of law. Let alone everything else you're going to hang for.'

'That ain't got nothing to do with you!'

Burton frowned, wondering briefly if Dodge had lost his marbles. 'The hell it doesn't! We found the mask in your cabin, Dodge.'

He strode outside and uncinched a saddle bag. When he returned, he was clutching the Phantom's mask.

'This was in your cabin,' he said coldly. 'You're a rapist and a killer. And you're going to hang for it.'

'So you and Blayloch are going to try to pin that on me, huh?' Dodge demanded.

'The evidence doesn't lie.'

'You and that stupid deputy lie,

though!' Dodge almost spat his words at Burton.

'You're wasting your breath, Dodge. You're a killer and everyone in this room knows that first hand. But you're going to pay for all of your crimes, not just the murder of Tim Beach.'

'I have the right to defend myself. You were all coming upon me with guns drawn. You were going to shoot me in my sleep!'

'Shut the hell up,' Martin Thompson muttered angrily.

'Put him in a cell,' Burton said, handing the keys to Otis Thompson.

The brothers shoved the prisoner into the hallway and opened the cell on the right side of the passage. Martin Thompson held Dodge while his brother cut the ropes from the man's wrists, then gave Dodge a forceful push into the cell and slammed the barred door closed behind him. They went back into the office and closed the heavy door to the cell block.

'How's Maynard doing?' Burton

asked O'Rourke.

'Well, he looks better than he did last time we saw him,' O'Rourke said. 'But I wouldn't necessarily say that he looks good.'

'He's lucky to be alive,' Burton remarked.

'Doc said he should be back on his feet in four or five days, but he's going to have to take it easy for a while after that.' O'Rourke removed his hat and sat down on the corner of Blayloch's desk. 'Sheriff might have to send another deputy out here to Oakridge until Maynard recovers.'

'Probably so,' said Burton. He turned to the Thompson brothers. 'Gentlemen, I thank you for your assistance in this matter.' He included O'Rourke in his glance. 'Y'all are probably aware that you'll be called upon to testify at Dodge's trial.' The men nodded. 'Anyway, I'm going to stay here today and spend the night. Frank, could I ask one more favor of you?'

'Of course.'

'Could you ride out to my place and let Annie know we're back? I'd like her to bring some fresh clothes and food over when she gets the chance.'

'I'll ride out there before I head home,' O'Rourke said.

'Thanks.'

Burton shook hands with all the men before they left, then watched them mount their horses and ride away.

★　★　★

Annie Burton arrived about an hour later in the couple's buggy. As her husband had requested, she brought food and clothing. Burton was eating some pie at Blayloch's desk and telling Annie about the hunt for the Dodge brothers when someone tapped at the office door.

'Come on in,' Burton called.

The door opened and the clerk from the telegraph office entered. He held out several telegrams for Burton, who began to examine them.

'There should be a temporary deputy arriving this afternoon from Eugene,' the telegrapher said. 'Maynard sent them a message the morning he was brought in from Deception Creek.'

'Good,' Burton said. 'I won't have to spend the night here after all.'

'You'll also notice something else,' the telegrapher said, pointing at the stack of telegrams in Burton's hand. 'The Dodge brothers are wanted for killing three men in a bank robbery up in Salem last week.'

Burton's eyebrows darted up with surprise and he searched for the telegram about the bank robbery. He found it and read it, as well as two more that had been sent to Oakridge with further information about the crime. It seemed the brothers were also suspected in a bank robbery up near Portland in which two people had been killed, including one woman.

'Tarnation,' Burton said under his breath. He looked up at Annie. 'They think the Dodges killed five people in their bank heists. And that's not including the Phantom murders and the killing of Tim Beach.'

'Killers,' Annie said, shaking her head. 'Stone cold killers.'

'You folks have a good day,' the telegrapher said as he exited out on to the boardwalk.

Burton was pensive. 'I'm going over to see Maynard after this new deputy arrives,' he said. He took another bite of his pie and re-examined the telegrams. 'It's too bad Dalton Dodge isn't here to be held accountable.'

'Sounds like he got his in the end,' Annie replied.

'I'm just glad Maynard's alive,' said Burton. 'He's going to have to get well soon. I'm sure they'll be sending a judge out here from Eugene for the trial within a day or two. They don't like to twiddle their thumbs when it comes to murder trials, especially when you throw in bank robbery, too. Maynard's going to be doing a lot of testifying.'

Annie gazed toward the cell block

door. She remembered the terror of the Phantom's thwarted attack and felt a cold shiver at how close she and her husband had come to being victims. Her mind troubled, she forced herself to focus on more practical issues.

'How're your feet doing?' she asked solicitously.

Burton pulled his chair out from behind the desk and removed his boots. Tattered, bloodstained rags were wrapped around his feet. He peeled them off.

'I put these on yesterday,' he explained as he dropped the rags on the floor.

The bottoms of his feet were still cut badly but were in better shape than Annie had expected them to be.

'I brought you that extra set of boots you bought last year,' she said.

'Oh, good.' He patted her hand. 'You always think of everything.'

She smiled. 'Somebody has to!' She rose and opened the door. 'I'll get those boots.'

As she turned to step on to the board-walk, a man appeared in the doorway.

He was tall, with lined brown skin and a bushy mustache. He removed his hat and smiled at Annie. Burton noticed the sunlight reflecting off the badge on his chest.

'Sorry, ma'am,' the man said as he moved out of Annie's way. He looked at Burton. 'Name's Matt Winstan. Sheriff sent me out here as deputy until Maynard's up and around.'

Burton rose and the men shook hands. 'I'm Ed Burton,' he said. 'I've been helping Maynard off and on for the last year or so, whenever he needs me. I used to be the marshal over in Fillmore. I led the posse and we captured Dodge in the mountains south of Deception Creek the day before yesterday.'

'Boy, y'all been busy!' Winstan said with a grin. 'Sheriff'll be real happy to hear that.' He hesitated. 'What about Dalton Dodge?'

'Dead. Died of blood loss after a shootout with me and Maynard. Well, either that or he got eaten by a black bear. We found some parts of him in a cave where he'd been hiding out. I don't think he was in any shape to get away if a bear found him while he was still alive. He'd lost a whole lot of blood by then and might have been dead already.'

'Don't really matter much,' said Winstan with a shrug.

'Emerson's been shot, too,' Burton added. 'Now that you're here I'll go fetch the doctor to take a look at him. I think the bullet passed through. He ain't said much about it.'

Winstan removed his hat and dropped it on Blayloch's desk. Then he took off his sheepskin coat and threw it across the back of a chair.

'He ate yet this morning?' he asked, pointing toward the cell block door.

'Not yet,' Burton said. 'I'll stop in at the café and have them send some food over.'

'Thank you. Could you ask them to send some food for me, too? I'm half starved.'

'I'll do that,' Burton said. Annie brought him his other pair of boots and he slipped them on. 'I'll be heading out now. You should be getting some food and a visit from the doc real soon.'

'Much obliged,' Winstan said with a good-natured wave.

They shook hands again and Burton followed Annie out on to the boardwalk.

'You heading home?' he asked.

'Not right away. I have to get some things at the store. I'll be home in a couple hours, I figure.'

He kissed her on the cheek and helped her up into the buggy.

'I'll probably be home before you are, then,' he said. He buttoned his coat. The misty air was the coldest it had been all year, he thought. 'I'll get a good fire going.'

'Thanks,' she said. 'Get some alcohol and clean up those feet.'

He promised to do so as they parted ways. He stopped in at the café and arranged to have food sent over for

Matt Winstan and Emerson Dodge. When he visited Doctor Rodgers, he learned that Maynard Blayloch was sleeping in the back room and unable to see anyone at the moment.

'He doing all right?' Burton asked.

'He could be worse,' said Rodgers. 'I wasn't sure he'd survive the first twenty-four hours, but he did. He's a tough young man.'

'Well, thank you for all you've done. We've got the man responsible for shooting him. Maynard will be able to see justice served.'

'I heard you found the Phantom's mask out at Dodge's cabin.'

Burton chuckled. 'Word travels fast here in Oakridge, don't it?'

'So it's true?'

'Yes, it is.'

'I'm just glad y'all found the man responsible,' Rodgers said. 'I've got two daughters myself, as you know. I wasn't happy knowing this Phantom character was prowling around at night.'

'I don't think you have to worry

about that anymore,' Burton said, pushing his hat down on his head and rising to leave. He wanted to ride home and maybe get an hour of sleep before Annie returned.

Burton asked the doctor to check out Dodge's wound, then mounted his horse and rode west out of town toward home.

★ ★ ★

The next day Maynard Blayloch felt well enough for Burton to visit him. The deputy sheriff was in a bed in the back room of Doctor Rodgers' house. He sat propped up on some pillows when Burton came into the room.

Blayloch was much thinner than his usual weight, and his skin looked dry like parchment. But he was alive.

'Maynard, how're you feeling?' Burton asked. He patted the lawman on the arm and sat down in a chair near the bed.

'I've felt better, I must admit,' Blayloch said. 'I'm just glad I'm still alive and kicking. That's thanks to you, Mr Burton. I won't forget it.'

'You'd have done the same for me, Maynard.'

'Maybe,' said Blayloch. 'But that's not how it played out.' He exhaled slowly, shaking his head at the memory of that night out at Emerson Dodge's place. 'I'm happy you got the bastard. You hear about the bank robberies up in Salem and Portland?'

'Yeah. He's made quite a name for himself. Left a lot of dead bodies behind, too.'

'Quite a pair, those Dodge boys.'

'You got Dalton pretty good out at the cabin the other night. He didn't make it very far into the mountains. His brother left him in a cave.'

'Well, I guess it saves us the time and cost of a trial for him. One less person we got to hang.'

'They should have a judge out here within a few days to hold the trial. If Emerson gets sentenced to hang they'll probably forgo a separate trial for the bank robberies and killings up north.'

Blayloch's face assumed a grave cast. 'Doctor Rodgers told me you found something out at the Dodge cabin.'

Burton nodded and unbuttoned his sheepskin. He pulled out the Phantom's mask and tossed it over on to Blayloch's lap. The mask itself seemed to have a malevolent aura about it, as if it embodied all the rage and violence of the Phantom in an inanimate form.

The deputy picked it up and looked it over, poking his fingers through the eye holes. He dropped it back on to his lap.

'Evidence don't get much more conclusive than that,' he said.

'He killed Tim Beach, too,' Burton said. 'I'm sure Frank O'Rourke told you that.'

'Yeah, he did. Damn sorry to hear that.'

'It's a shame, that's for sure.'

Burton put his hands on the arms of his chair and pushed himself to his feet. 'Well, Maynard, I'd better head along.

You get some more rest. Let me know if I can help you with anything, or if Annie can.'

Blayloch raised a hand and smiled.

'Thanks, Mr Burton. I'll be talking to you soon.'

Minutes later, Burton rode out of town beneath darkening skies.

11

Judge George G. Gilman arrived from Eugene five days after the posse returned. Maynard Blayloch, who was on his feet at last, met the judge as the latter dismounted in the street outside the deputy's office. Gilman was a short, thin man, meticulously dressed despite his muddy boots. He had thick white hair and a bushy white beard that came down to a point beneath his gaunt features. Blayloch figured he was somewhere around seventy years old.

The old man had chosen to ride alone from Eugene, a few hours to the west, in the cold morning air, but he seemed as fresh as a daisy to Blayloch's eyes. There was a no-nonsense intensity about the man.

'You must be Deputy Blayloch,' Gilman said briskly. He didn't smile.

'Yes, sir,' Blayloch said.

He put out his hand, and the judge shook it firmly and quickly before releasing it.

'I want to see the prisoner first thing,' Gilman said.

'Yes, sir,' Blayloch answered.

People tended to use those two words a lot around Judge Gilman.

Blayloch opened the door to his office and admitted him, then opened the door to the cell block and stepped aside.

Gilman removed his hat and walked into the passageway, where he stopped before Emerson Dodge's cell. The prisoner had been dozing, but he awakened and sat up on his cot when he heard the door open.

'What's your name?' Gilman demanded.

'Emerson Dodge.'

'You been getting regular meals?'

'Yeah.'

Gilman's nostrils flared. 'What?' he asked sharply.

'Um — yes, sir. Regular meals.'

'You seen your attorney?'

'Yes, sir. This morning.'

Gilman nodded, satisfied. 'Fine. Your trial will start as soon as both counselors are prepared to present their cases.'

Dodge's mouth opened and he started to say something, but Judge Gilman turned and walked out of the cell block, slamming the door shut behind him.

★　★　★

A few hours after the judge got to Oakridge, an assistant district attorney arrived on a stage coach. He alighted in front of the café and took his luggage from the driver.

Oakridge's sole local attorney had agreed to serve as defense counsel for Emerson Dodge. The two lawyers took several days assembling their cases, taking statements from witnesses, and occasionally visiting a crime scene.

Five days after the prosecutor's arrival, all parties were ready to move forward with the trial, which Judge Gilman convened at eight o'clock on a drizzling Monday morning in the large room upstairs from Maynard Blayloch's office and the jail. A staircase on the side of the building led up to the door of the makeshift court room. A table had been placed at the front of the room for the judge; two small desks faced the table, one for the prosecution and one for the defense. Behind these desks were several rows of chairs that the judge had ordered placed in the room for any locals who wanted to observe the trial. From the first day, all the chairs were filled with spectators.

Judge Gilman banged his gavel commandingly on the table and swept a flinty glare around the room. The excited chatter of the spectators ceased immediately. After bringing the court to order, Gilman briefly outlined the essentials of the case, which, he noted pointedly, was concerned only with the crimes that had been committed in Lane County. This precluded the crimes that the Dodge brothers had allegedly committed in Salem and Portland.

Gilman noted also that Emerson Dodge had waived his right to a jury trial and had chosen instead to have the judge himself hand down the decision. Gilman didn't explain that Dodge was convinced that a jury comprised of Oakridge residents would be hopelessly prejudiced against him, not only for the Phantom attacks (which he still denied) but also for the death of Tim Beach, a popular man around those parts. Gilman had been a judge in the county for more than thirty years, and even Dodge was aware of his reputation for scrupulous fairness before the law.

Gilman announced that the trial would begin with the evidence in the death of Tim Beach before addressing the rapes and murders committed by the Phantom.

The prosecutor's name was Tyler Hatch. He was a young man, no older than twenty-seven or twenty-eight, Burton thought. He was short and somewhat stout, with slicked-back black hair and a pink, clean-shaven baby face. Despite his youthful appearance, he had a remarkable command of the courtroom, with a courteous but determined manner that had already proven very effective in the man's relatively short career. Burton enjoyed watching him work.

Hatch laid out the case against Dodge in the murder of Tim Beach. The judge swore in all the members of the posse, who recounted how the defendant had shot Beach on the mountainside south of Deception Creek. The testimony was straightforward and Dodge's lawyer, an elderly man named Arthur Nickson who hadn't tried a case in over twenty years, only bothered to ask a few perfunctory questions, none of which implied that the members of the posse were lying. Rather, he suggested that Dodge could have been disoriented when he woke up and discovered the posse surrounding him. The shooting of Tim Beach, Nickson hinted mildly, may have been more instinctual and accidental than intentional.

The line of reasoning was a weak one

in Burton's view. He was pleased when he saw Nickson sit back down without attempting to push the argument further.

Throughout the proceedings, Emerson Dodge sat with his wrists and ankles bound at the defense's desk. He said nothing, his jaw set with defiance, a sullen expression on his face. Occasionally he rolled his eyes or shook his head at something the prosecutor or one of the witnesses said. His disdain for the entire process was unalloyed.

The portion of the trial devoted to the murder of Tim Beach was concluded by lunchtime on the first day. Judge Gilman called a recess and promptly descended the stairs outside before crossing the muddy street to the café. Maynard Blayloch and Matt Winstan, who had decided to stay in town for the trial, took Dodge downstairs and locked him back in his cell.

The trial resumed exactly one hour later. The judge was nothing if not efficient.

There wasn't an empty seat in the room, and more than a dozen other locals were crowded into the corners and behind the chairs at the back. The trial of Emerson Dodge was the most exciting thing to hit Oakridge since a US senator had delivered a speech there a few years before.

Gilman banged his gavel and gave a few instructions to the attorneys. Then Tyler Hatch laid out the state's evidence against Dodge in the Phantom attacks.

'The record will show that the first Phantom attacks took place six years ago now,' Hatch said in his smooth voice. 'Interestingly enough, Emerson Dodge happened to be living in Oakridge at the very same time that these nefarious crimes began, in the summer of 1874. The record will also show that the crimes mysteriously stopped a few months later — precisely when the defendant left the area.'

Hatch paced slowly back and forth before the judge's table as he spoke, his right forefinger pressed thoughtfully against his chin.

'Your Honor, I would like to observe that at no time between 1874 and 1879 did the Phantom strike,' he continued. 'During this period, Emerson Dodge was living elsewhere, mostly in Salem with his brother. But when Buck Dodge, his uncle and a widely respected man in these parts for many decades, died last year, he left his property to his oldest nephew. Emerson Dodge moved back to Deception Creek, into his uncle's old cabin. And what happened shortly thereafter? The Phantom struck again, after years of inactivity.'

Hatch stopped pacing and stood up straight, his fingers laced across his bulging belly. 'I would submit, Your Honor, that this is no mere coincidence. I would also submit that there is no conspiracy afoot among the fine, moral, God-fearing citizens of this town to place the blame for these crimes on an innocent man.' The prosecutor removed a silk handkerchief from the inside pocket of his coat and wiped the thick layer of sweat from his brow and upper lip. 'Nay, Your Honor. Emerson Dodge is not the victim here, but rather the transgressor. He is the Phantom.'

Hatch called several witnesses, including Pete Dexter, Everett Bickham, and Mike Sheed. Burton was surprised that all three men had agreed to testify, although he realized they ultimately had no choice. Neither Judge Gilman nor Tyler Hatch thought it necessary for any of the women who had been raped by the Phantom to testify, and Arthur Nickson was too old, too tired, and too dejected by the force of the evidence against his client to argue otherwise.

The witnesses all agreed that the Phantom was approximately the same height and weight as Emerson Dodge, who also shared the predator's blue eyes.

Judge Gilman brought the day's proceedings to an end at precisely five o'clock that afternoon.

'We will continue in the morning, picking up where we left off today. Mr

Hatch, you will be calling witnesses in the morning?'

Hatch nodded. 'Yes, sir. I will be calling Deputy Sheriff Maynard Blayloch and Mr Edward Burton.'

'Fair enough. I expect those men to be ready to testify first thing, then. This court is adjourned.' He banged his gavel resoundingly and left the room without any further ado. The spectators could hear his boots thumping down the wooden steps outside.

* * *

The next morning, Burton got up early. He let Annie sleep while he made some coffee for them both. She awakened and sipped her coffee while he made some eggs and bacon. After serving her and eating, he cleaned up, dressed, and rode into Oakridge.

Maynard Blayloch's office door was open as Burton hitched his horse out front. Spectators were already streaming up the steps to get a seat.

'Good morning, Maynard,' Burton said, leaning in the door.

Blayloch waved and got up. He walked out of the office and locked the door behind him. Matt Winstan had already taken Emerson Dodge upstairs.

'All ready?' Blayloch asked.

Burton nodded. 'As ready as I'll ever be.'

They climbed up the stairs and took their places in the front row of chairs. Burton removed his watch from his pocket and checked the time. It was exactly eight o'clock. The door opened and Judge Gilman strode in. He removed his hat, sat down, and hammered the court to order.

'Call your first witness for the day, Mr Hatch,' the judge ordered.

'Your Honor, the state calls Deputy Maynard Blayloch.'

The deputy crossed to the chair beside the judge's table and Gilman swore him in.

'Deputy Blayloch, can you tell us about your involvement in the attempt to capture the Phantom, and how you came to believe that Emerson Dodge and the Phantom are one and the same?'

Blayloch sniffed and ran a hand over his neatly combed hair.

'Well, I've been a deputy sheriff here in Oakridge for . . . I guess five years now. I was born and raised around here, so I remember the first round of attacks by the Phantom, although I was not an officer of the law at that time. I did not become involved in trying to apprehend him until about a year ago, when he began to break into homes and rape women again.'

There was a tense silence in the room. Burton shifted his eyes to Emerson Dodge. The prisoner sat glaring at Blayloch, his fists clenched so hard that his knuckles were white. Ed Burton wasn't a man who spooked easily, but something about the manner in which Dodge was looking at Maynard Blayloch made the hair on the back of his neck bristle.

'So you have been leading the investigation ever since the Phantom reappeared last year?'

'Yes,' confirmed Blayloch. Then, flustered slightly, he corrected himself. 'Well — apart from when Ed Burton led the posse after the Dodge brothers out past Deception Creek.'

Tyler Hatch started pacing again, as was his wont, and his finger once more found its way to his chin as he formulated his thoughts.

'How did you start to focus on the Dodges?'

'We didn't really focus on both of the Dodge brothers, sir. We were only investigating Emerson. We ran into Dalton after the Phantom tried to attack the Burtons. He and Emerson came out of that cabin shooting.' He examined a spot on his pants for a few seconds, recalling his brush with death. 'We started looking into Emerson when he showed up at that community meeting at the church last year. He was acting real strange. Mr Burton noticed it, and I noticed it, too.'

'At that juncture, you had no inkling that Mr Dodge might be involved in other criminal activity, including murder?' Hatch asked.

Arthur Nickson began to rise slowly to his feet.

Before Nickson could object, Blayloch said, 'No, sir. Didn't know about that.'

Dodge's lawyer sat back down.

'What else implicated Emerson Dodge, in your opinion?'

'He's pretty much the same size as the Phantom, according to witnesses,' Blayloch said. 'He lived here at the time of both series of attacks. And he's got blue eyes. Also, he was real hostile to me and Mr Burton whenever we tried to talk to him.'

'Tell us about the night you were shot, please.'

'It started with the Phantom trying to get into Ed Burton's house. He chased him away and then came and got me. We went out to the Dodge place just to see what was going on out there.

Emerson Dodge had been gone a spell, supposedly up at his brother's spread in Salem, but when we got there, the brothers came out shooting. I got shot, and then Mr Burton put a posse together and gave chase. He found the mask in a bedroom in the Dodge cabin.'

Emerson Dodge spat on the floor. 'These are lies!' he screamed. 'You're a goddamn liar, Maynard!'

Judge Gilman pounded his gavel as a murmur spread through the spectators.

'Silence!' he growled. The response was immediate. His eyes swiveled to the prisoner. 'One more stunt like that from you and I'll have you removed.' He pointed his gavel at Dodge. 'This is a court of law. Don't forget that.'

Tyler Hatch concluded his examination of the witness. Nickson rose and asked a few perfunctory questions, then sat back down.

Hatch called Burton to the stand and Gilman swore him in.

'Mr Burton, can you say a little

something about your experience as a lawman?' Hatch asked.

'I was the town marshal in Fillmore, Oregon for fourteen years,' Burton said. 'In that time I handled hundreds of investigations, from horse theft and arson to rape and murder.'

'And why are you no longer the marshal in Fillmore, Mr Burton?'

Burton's face darkened. 'I — uh, I decided to resign last year after a real ugly murder investigation.' He shrugged. 'Had enough, I guess you could say.'

Hatch opened a valise on his desk, every eye in the courtroom riveted on him. He reached inside the valise and carefully removed the Phantom's mask. A gasp went through the crowd, and several people stood up to get a better look. Even Emerson Dodge leaned forward to look at it. Then he sat back and shook his head.

Hatch walked Burton through his involvement in the Phantom investigation, including his part in the organization of the nightly patrols. Burton recounted his suspicions about Emerson Dodge, the attempt on his life near Deception Creek on the night of the community meeting, and the sudden reappearance of the Phantom at his home after a year without any attacks.

Hatch went over the shooting of Maynard Blayloch and the subsequent escape by the Dodge brothers. Then he asked about the mask.

'I found the mask just before me and the posse headed into the mountains,' Burton explained. 'The back door to the Dodge cabin had been left open and I decided to take a quick look around before shutting it. It was on a chair in one of the bedrooms. They must have been in such a hurry to get out of there that they forgot to take it with them. Or at least Emerson forgot. I don't know that his brother had anything to do with the Phantom attacks.'

'You're a liar, too, Burton!' screamed Dodge, who spat again on the plank floor.

Burton stared back at him, his face impassive.

Judge Gilman pounded the table once, this time with his fist rather than his gavel.

'Deputy Winstan,' he said, his voice loud and authoritative. 'Take this prisoner back to his cell. He can remain there for the rest of the day's proceedings.' His frigid eyes were locked on Dodge.

Matt Winstan rose from his chair in the front row. His big hand gripped Dodge by the back of the shirt and yanked the man to his feet.

'C'mon, smartass,' Winstan said.

Dodge didn't say anything more; instead, he glared hard at Burton until the deputy got him outside and closed the door.

'Mr Hatch, do you have any further questions for the witness?' asked the judge.

'I do not.'

'Very well, then — Mr Nickson, what about you?'

'No, sir,' said the elderly attorney.

Burton thought he looked like he regretted coming out of retirement for the case.

Gilman dismissed Burton from the witness chair. As there was no further evidence to present or any further witnesses being called, the judge moved to closing arguments. Hatch addressed the court for nearly a half hour, making an eloquent and at times passionate case for conviction and execution.

Nickson followed and spoke very briefly. He was resigned to losing the case and probably thought his client was guilty anyway. However, Burton found the man's arguments more persuasive and effective than he had anticipated, although he remained unconvinced. Finding the mask in Dodge's cabin had sealed the deal for him.

Judge Gilman announced that he would have a verdict ready in the morning and adjourned the court. Burton went home that night and spent a quiet evening with Annie. She had chosen not to attend the trial. The details were too disturbing for her. After supper, Burton stoked the fire. He couldn't help but looking out the living room window to the spot in the trees where he had spotted the Phantom lurking in the shadows. It had been less than two weeks ago, but for Burton it felt like a lifetime. He felt a deep sense of relief knowing that the man responsible had been captured.

The next morning he was in the front row again when Judge Gilman started the proceedings. He had several sheets of paper on the desk in front of him — his verdict. He had written it down in his room at the boarding house the night before. He read it aloud, and the tension in the room was almost palpable.

' . . . and therefore,' he concluded, 'this court finds the defendant, Emerson Farnsworth Dodge, guilty of the crimes of murder and rape. The sentence is death by hanging, to be carried out within the town limits of Oakridge no later than seventy-two hours from the present moment. That concludes this trial.'

Gilman hit the table one last time with his gavel and left the room, taking his written decision with him.

Emerson Dodge stared silently ahead, his face inscrutable.

★　★　★

Men began constructing the scaffold that same afternoon.

The sound of the steadily pounding hammers was ominous. Burton had stayed in town for a few hours after the verdict, talking to Blayloch and Winstan. Tyler Hatch stopped in Blayloch's office and shook hands with Burton and the deputy.

'Thank you, men, for your invaluable testimony,' he said. 'Justice has been served, in no small part thanks to your help. No longer will the women of Oakridge have to fear a madman.'

Burton and Blayloch acknowledged his thanks. The prosecutor rode out of town soon after, accompanied by Matt Winstan. Maynard Blayloch had assured the latter that he felt well enough to handle his duties without assistance. Winstan had been skeptical but he didn't want to argue.

'Suit yourself, Maynard,' he said. 'But you take it easy, y'hear?'

Judge Gilman stayed in Oakridge for the hanging, which took place two days later. The scaffold had been completed with the help of four skilled carpenters from the local area. It stood in a vacant field at the end of Main Street, about a hundred yards from the drunkards' shack.

Burton rode into town to witness the execution. It was another overcast and windy morning in the late Oregon fall. He was startled by the size of the crowd, which seemed to include every single resident of Oakridge and the surrounding area, including children of various ages. Their faces were somber as they stood in the muddy lot. Burton spotted Judge Gilman standing at the front of the crowd.

Heads turned as Maynard Blayloch

rode toward the scaffold. Emerson Dodge, hands tied, was on a horse beside Blayloch, who led the condemned man's mount by the reins. When they pulled leather behind the scaffold, Hank Kirby stepped forward and assisted the deputy in taking Dodge down from his horse.

They tied the horses to a pole on the scaffold and led Dodge up the stairs to the platform. The wind was blowing hard as he stood there, his predatory eyes scanning the faces below him. His thick, straight hair was swept down over his forehead in the gusty air.

Kirby and Blayloch took Dodge by the shoulders and moved him atop the trapdoor.

'Do you have any last words before your sentence is carried out?' Blayloch asked.

'Yes,' Dodge said, his tone defiant. 'I want to say that this was a crooked trial and I've been falsely convicted. So y'all can go to hell!' He spat one last time, for emphasis. He twisted around to face

Maynard Blayloch. 'Let's get this over with, you pious son of a bitch.'

Blayloch nodded to Kirby, who pulled a hood over Dodge's head. The deputy slipped the noose over the man's neck, then tightened it behind his right ear. Kirby and Blayloch stepped back from the trapdoor.

Dodge stood shivering in the wind, which sent ripples across his shirt. Burton knew it wasn't the cold that caused the man's shivering.

Maynard Blayloch pulled the lever and the trapdoor fell open. Dodge fell through and the rope was suddenly taut, breaking his neck with a loud snapping sound. The rope creaked as his body swung back and forth, the head lolling first sideways and then forward at an unnatural angle.

The crowd began to disperse after a minute. Burton helped Kirby and Blayloch cut down the body, which they put over the dead man's horse for the brief sojourn to the cemetery behind the church.

12

There were no more Phantom attacks after the execution of Emerson Dodge.

Life returned to normal in Oakridge. No longer did families barricade themselves in their homes, guns at the ready. No longer were men looked at with suspicion by their neighbors.

Ed and Annie Burton's lives settled down to a placid routine. Burton was able to devote more time to managing the property. As during the period following the end of the patrols, he saw much less of Maynard Blayloch.

Burton was chopping wood on a cold January morning when he observed Hank Kirby emerge from the forest and ride across the yard. Burton wiped sweat off his brow and stood watching the rider approach.

'Hello, Hank,' he said. 'What brings you out here?'

'Morning, Mr Burton,' Kirby said. Burton still hadn't been able to talk the rancher into calling him by his first name. 'How are you doing?'

'Fine, fine.' Burton sighed and put his ax down. 'I have a feeling we're going to have snow before too long.'

Kirby glanced at the forested ridges that surrounded Burton's property.

'I hope not,' he said. 'I've got too much work to do without having to deal with a bunch of snow. But I reckon you're right.' He cleared his throat. 'I came out to ask if you would like to do some hunting this weekend. Me and Maynard were thinking about spending a couple days in the mountains south of the Dodge place.'

Burton's face reflected surprise. 'Have you been there since the posse brought Emerson Dodge back?'

'No, I haven't. It's good hunting, though. Maynard was going to come and ask you if you'd like to come along, but he got called to Eugene for some kind of official business.'

'What day you two planning on heading out?' Burton asked.

'Saturday morning. It might be just one night, maybe two. Depends on how lucky we are.'

'Sure, I can do that. Wouldn't mind getting me some fresh venison.'

'Good,' Kirby said. 'We're planning on meeting at my place around seven.'

The men chatted for a few more minutes and then Kirby rode out. Two mornings later Burton met Blayloch as he turned to ride up the private trail to Hank Kirby's property. They greeted each other and rode parallel through the trees toward the large cabin up ahead, quickly catching up on what they had been doing since the last time they spoke.

Kirby met them on the porch and invited them in for breakfast and coffee. Burton had already eaten, although he somehow found room for a few of Mrs Kirby's waffles and two cups of coffee. Blayloch was ravenously hungry, as usual. It was almost half after eight before the three riders headed west for Deception Creek. Kirby brought along a pack mule.

They turned south on to the trail leading past the Dodge property. They pulled leather in the yard, feeling mixed emotions. The cabin seemed more run down than it had just a few months before, and someone had thrown a rock through the grimy front window.

'Either of you been out here lately?' Burton asked.

Kirby and Blayloch shook their heads.

'I guess Dalton Dodge's widow owns it now,' said Blayloch. 'Don't look like she's taken much of an interest in it.'

'That's a shame,' said Kirby. 'Buck Dodge would have been real broke up to know no one wanted his spread.'

A few minutes later they rode on across the pasture toward the mountains.

'You know, I haven't mentioned this to anyone yet,' Blayloch said suddenly, 'but I'm thinking I might want to move on, find myself a new line of work.'

Burton and Kirby looked at the deputy with surprise.

'Well, I'd never have figured,' Kirby remarked. 'How long you been thinking like that?'

'For a while now. You know, I can handle the routine aspects of keeping the peace, but when you have to deal with rapes and murders it sometimes makes you wonder why you picked this job.'

Burton chuckled sympathetically. 'Believe me — I know what you're saying. I don't think there was a single year that went by in Fillmore when I didn't swear I was going to quit.'

'What would you do instead?' Kirby asked.

'Don't know yet,' said Blayloch. 'Got a couple things in mind as possibilities. I'd kind of like to get out of Oakridge and see the world a little. You know, I've never been to San Francisco. I thought maybe I'd go there and check things out, see what life is like in a big city.'

'You wouldn't regret visiting San Francisco,' Burton said. 'I've only been there once but it's quite a place, Maynard.'

'It was just an idea. I got some money saved up, so I could do a lot of different things. I just got to pick something.'

'So you're pretty sure you are going to quit?'

Blayloch nodded. 'Yeah, I think so. The job just ain't much fun anymore. But who knows — maybe I'll get the itch to be a lawman again someday, after I've had a break and done something else.' He gestured toward Burton. 'Look at you, Mr Burton. You still got the bug.'

'Quitting is harder than it looks,' Burton admitted. 'At least it was for me.'

The trio rode at a moderate pace, not wanting to labor the horses. They began the ascent into the mountains shortly before dusk and then made camp in a clearing off the trail. Normally Kirby and Blayloch, both of whom had done some hunting in the range in years past, would have wanted to hole up in the first of the mountain caves, but that convenient shelter was no longer an option. Instead it had become a tomb for what remained of Dalton Dodge.

Kirby made a fire and boiled coffee. They had decided to rough it with only dry meat and cold biscuits on the first night. Burton had eaten so much that morning that he still wasn't particularly hungry.

After eating supper and drinking a little whiskey from a bottle in Blayloch's saddle-bag, the men rolled up in their blankets and swiftly fell asleep, lulled by the warmth of the fire.

* * *

The next morning they broke camp early and soon had luck finding prey. Kirby took down a deer before noon and Burton stalked a large buck for more than an hour before shooting it not far from the cave where Dalton Dodge had died. Blayloch trailed along with Burton while Kirby took his own deer back to the camp.

The sun was starting to set on the horizon when Burton and Blayloch returned to camp. Burton had bagged his quarry and Blayloch had a small deer to show for his efforts. They quickly field dressed the animals.

'Annie'll be happy to see me when I come home with this,' Burton said proudly.

Kirby had already begun cutting poles to make a travois to haul the dead deer back to Oakridge. They had just completed that task when Blayloch stood up, feeling the pockets of his coat with a frown. Then he looked around the camp.

'What the matter?' Kirby asked, finishing up with the travois poles.

'Left my damn field glasses up by the cave,' said Blayloch, irritated with himself. 'I'm going to have to go back for them.' He frowned. 'I'm sorry,

223

fellers — you go on ahead of me. I got those field glasses from my pa and I can't leave them behind.'

Burton waved an understanding hand and said, 'Don't worry about it, Maynard. We'll wait for you.'

'I'll make it real quick,' Blayloch said, already mounting his sorrel.

Kirby was ready to tie the travois poles together.

'We got any more rope?' he asked. He put his hands in the small of his back and leaned backward, stretching his tired muscles with a groan.

Blayloch pointed at his ditty bag, which lay on the ground beside his bedroll.

'I got rope in there,' he said. 'I'll be back quick as I can.'

Burton and Kirby waved at Blayloch and the deputy rode out of camp. He spurred his horse and picked up speed, soon disappearing in the trees as the trail turned a corner.

Burton walked over to the ditty bag and opened it. Inside was a long coiled rope, with shorter lengths of rope underneath. He pulled the coiled rope out of the bag and suddenly felt a cold shock run through his body. His scalp tingled and a feeling of dread filled his throat and stomach.

He held up the end of the rope and looked at the knot that Maynard Blayloch had tied there. Only once in his life had he seen that specific knot. It was distinctive, tied from multiple loops that formed a diamond shape when pulled tight. He could remember the precise moment he had seen it. A diamond knot had been used to bind Bob and Cindy Ballard in their bed, just before the Phantom crushed their skulls with a large chunk of firewood.

* * *

Maynard Blayloch was tired by the time he rode back into camp.

The travois had been completed and placed on the pack mule. The three deer were loaded on to it and tied down for the trip back to Oakridge. Burton and Kirby were standing near the fire, drinking coffee.

'I found them!' Blayloch announced.

'Glad to hear it,' Burton said.

Kirby said nothing.

Blayloch rode over to a small sapling, to which he tied his reins after dismounting.

'Boy, I can already taste that venison!' he said, looking eagerly at the travois. 'You got any more of that coffee?' After a moment he realized that neither Burton nor Kirby had answered him. He turned toward them and froze where he stood.

Ed Burton was holding his Navy Colt at waist level. It was pointed directly at Blayloch's chest.

'What the hell — ' Blayloch began, but Burton cut him off.

'Don't make any fast moves, Maynard,' he said steadily. 'I don't want to shoot you, but rest assured I will if I have to.' The expression on his face was grave.

Blayloch flicked his glance to Kirby, who had also drawn his pistol and trained it on the deputy.

'Take your pistol and drop it,' Burton said.

Blayloch's voice trembled slightly as he asked, 'What's going on here, fellers?'

'You know what's going on,' Burton said. 'You're the Phantom. You set up Emerson Dodge. He was a killer anyway, yes — but he wasn't the Phantom.'

'What're you talking about?' Blayloch asked. He was trying hard to seem casual, as if this were some sort of silly mistake they would all be laughing about soon.

'You tied that diamond knot on the Ballards. I'd never seen that kind of knot anywhere in my life until we were investigating the Phantom. I asked Hank and he said the same thing. You must have forgotten that you'd used that knot on the rope in your ditty bag.' Blayloch tried to respond but again Burton stopped him. 'You better drop that pistol. I won't say it again.'

Blayloch dragged his pistol from its holster and tossed it into the grass before him.

'Put your hands up,' Burton said.

Blayloch obeyed. His glibness had evaporated.

'You slippery bastard,' snarled Burton. 'It was you all along. That was you outside my house that night. You done denying it?'

Blayloch realized the game was up; Burton could see it on the man's face.

'You know, you're about the same size as Emerson Dodge. Blue eyes, too. It must have been pretty easy for you to set him up once I told you I had suspicions about him.' He exhaled slowly through clenched teeth as he pondered the extent of Blayloch's deception. 'You know, I've been wondering how you planted the mask in Dodge's cabin. And then I remembered — I pulled you into his kitchen out of the rain. You had that mask in your coat, didn't you, Maynard? And I'm sure you told yourself that Emerson Dodge had it coming, because he was a killer anyway. But you're a killer, too. You were the one who shot at me out at Deception Creek after the meeting at the church. You were going to kill me and Annie that night at my place, weren't you?'

Still Blayloch said nothing. The totality of his exposure seemed to have robbed him of the power of speech.

Hank Kirby kept his pistol fixed on Blayloch.

'Hard to believe, Maynard,' he said simply. But believe it he did.

'Raping women wasn't good enough anymore?' Burton asked.

Dark emotions assailed him as he watched the man whom he had helped, respected, and praised in both public and private. The face behind that mask had been Maynard Blayloch's. Still Burton's mind seemed to fight against this realization.

But Blayloch's silence was deafening.

'Hank, tie him up, will you?' Burton asked. He had to attend to practical matters.

Kirby holstered his Colt and walked toward Blayloch, whose hands were still raised. Blayloch's eyes stared off into the distance, as if he were disassociating himself from the events unfolding before him.

Kirby paused to kick Blayloch's pistol further off into the grass. He pulled a length of rope from his pocket, then reached up and gripped Blayloch's left wrist and began turning him around.

Blayloch let Kirby turn him part of the way, then struck with a swiftness that left the rancher unable to respond. He grabbed Kirby's shirtfront with his left hand and pulled the man in close to him, swinging his right arm down at the same time. The derringer slipped from his sleeve into his right hand, and he fired both barrels into Kirby's chest at point-blank range. Kirby made a grotesque wheezing sound, trying to draw a breath, and blood streamed from the side of his mouth as his eyes glazed over.

Kirby stood between Burton and

Blayloch, obscuring the former's view. By the time Burton realized what had happened, Blayloch had already pulled Kirby's pistol out of its holster and was firing at Burton, who leapt behind Kirby's horse, feeling an intense burning sensation in the back of his left thigh. Blayloch's bullet had hit him in the leg.

He hit the ground hard, returning fire with three wild shots from between the startled mare's legs, then rolled through some brush and down a small embankment. Blayloch's bullets darted past him, but he scrambled toward the trees despite having had the wind knocked out of him. He gasped for air as he ran.

Blayloch raced around the dying campfire and fired toward the trees where Burton had disappeared. He stepped through the grass and picked up his own pistol, which Kirby had kicked aside. Pistol in hand, he started running in pursuit.

Two bullets blasted out from the

forest, thumping into the ground just ahead of Blayloch's feet. Blayloch crouched and hurled himself just inside the edge of the woods. Another bullet struck a tree above his head.

Blayloch lay still behind the tree. In the aftermath of the last shot he could hear the sound of branches snapping and rustling as Burton moved further into the forest somewhere to his right, a few dozen yards away.

Burton kept his legs in motion as long as he could and then, when the pain from the bullet wound in his thigh became too great, he collapsed on to the ground, not nearly as far from Blayloch as he would have liked.

His chest heaving, he rolled over on to his back and dragged himself a few yards further on his elbows before he could go no more. He lay on his back in the moist grass. He knew he had already fired all six of the shots in his Navy Colt, yet he still felt compelled to break open the gun and check the empty cylinder, just to make sure. It was empty, like he knew it would be. He tried to stand up again, but his leg seemed to be paralyzed and he fell back on to the ground.

The eerie stillness was broken by the voice of Maynard Blayloch.

'Mr Burton, I know you can hear me,' the killer called. Blayloch let his words sink in for a minute before continuing. 'I want you to know a couple things. I never wanted it to come to this. I get these urges, you see. I've been getting them ever since I was a kid. I try to fight them. I swear I do. But they're . . . stronger than I am.'

He was silent again for several seconds, and Burton could hear the sounds of movement in the forest. Unhurried, methodical movement.

'I didn't even want to get you involved,' Blayloch went on. His voice sounded strange to Burton. Blayloch had to know that Burton was out of bullets, yet the man's voice didn't sound triumphant; more than anything else, it seemed sad. 'The sheriff is the one who insisted. He'd read the articles in the newspaper about that case of yours from a couple years ago.'

The voice was closer now.

'I meant to stop last year. I swear I did. You believe me, don't you? I don't blame you if you don't. I don't know why I went out there to your house that night. I'm sorry about that. I shouldn't have done it. Sometimes I wish you hadn't missed when you shot at me.'

Burton could see Blayloch now, coming through the trees toward him, his silhouette outlined by the moonlight. Burton cursed quietly at his own inability to stand. He looked around for a fallen tree limb or anything he could use to defend himself. There was nothing.

Blayloch was now ten feet away from Burton, who could see the outline of the pistol in the man's right hand. Burton grunted and threw his gun at Blayloch, who deflected it with his forearm. His face grimaced with pain for a moment, and then he halted a few feet away.

They faced each other. Burton's

breathing was labored and his useless left leg throbbed with pain. At that moment, however, he was oblivious to his physical ailments. He was preparing for his own death. His mind turned to Annie, and then to his two sons who had died years before . . .

Blayloch raised the gun and pointed it at Burton, who braced himself for the shot.

'I didn't want it to be like this,' Blayloch said again, his voice softer this time.

Burton looked down the barrel. Never had he been this defenseless, this close to oblivion. But the bullet didn't come. Seconds passed, and yet Blayloch didn't fire.

Burton's eyes moved from the barrel and focused on Maynard Blayloch's face. The blue eyes stared back. The gun trembled in his hand for a moment, still pointed directly at Burton. Then he pulled it back.

In one fluid motion, Blayloch lifted the pistol toward his own head. He brought up his other hand and gripped the handle with it, inserting the barrel into his mouth. Then he squeezed the trigger and the gun fired, blasting a stream of blood and brains out of the back of his head into the trees behind him.

13

Limping slightly as he made his way up the cemetery hill, Ed Burton stopped in front of a grave with a small gray tombstone. On it was written: *Henry Joseph Kirby, 1824-1880*. Burton's face was ashen as he looked down at the grave.

He had been unable to attend Kirby's funeral, and it had taken nearly six weeks to recover from the gunshot wound to his leg. He had been forced to accept the fact that he would walk with a limp for the rest of his life. His innate determination helped speed up his recuperation. After getting back on his feet, it took another two weeks until he felt up to riding. The first place he had gone was the cemetery, to pay his respects to Hank Kirby.

He looked up and observed the heavy dark clouds that swirled above. Annie had been predicting a storm for three days now. It looked like her prediction was going to come true after all.

The wind blew some leaves across the grave and stirred the grass. Burton turned when he heard the sound of an approaching horse.

Deputy Matt Winstan was riding up the narrow trail past the cemetery fence to where Burton was standing. He nodded in greeting, and Burton smiled wanly.

'Morning, Matt.'

Winstan dismounted. 'Good morning, Mr Burton. I'm glad to see you're up and about.'

'Thanks. I'm pretty glad, too.'

'I'll bet,' agreed Winstan. He looked down at the tombstone and his face became somber. 'Damn shame,' he said quietly. 'Hank Kirby was a good man.'

'Yes, he was.'

The men were quiet for a minute.

'They buried Bob and Cindy Ballard up there,' Winstan said finally, gesturing up the hill to a large tombstone underneath a maple tree.

Burton looked where Winstan had pointed. He shook his head almost imperceptibly. He felt a strong urge to be on his way.

'So they assigned you out here as deputy?' he asked, changing the subject.

'Yeah, at least for the time being.'

Burton and Winstan turned and began walking down the hill toward the gate, Winstan leading his horse by the reins. On the far side of the rise was a withered old birch tree. Winstan pointed at it.

'That's where they buried Maynard,' he said. 'Beside Emerson Dodge.'

Burton said nothing. He had spotted the two unmarked graves as he rode into the cemetery. Without being told, he knew who was buried there.

Burton's horse was tied to the cemetery gate. He reached up and unlooped the reins from the post.

'Well, I got to head back to town,' Winstan said. 'I seen you as I was riding by and thought I'd say hello.'

'Thanks, Matt,' Burton said, managing a tight smile.

Winstan mounted and rode down the trail toward Oakridge. Burton's horse snorted and he patted its neck, talking to it quietly. Even the horse wants to get out of here, he thought.

He turned back, his eyes sweeping over the cemetery one last time. Then he mounted and rode home.

We do hope that you have enjoyed reading this large print book.

Did you know that all of our titles are available for purchase?

We publish a wide range of high quality large print books including:
Romances, Mysteries, Classics
General Fiction
Non Fiction and Westerns

Special interest titles available in large print are:
The Little Oxford Dictionary
Music Book, Song Book
Hymn Book, Service Book

Also available from us courtesy of Oxford University Press:
Young Readers' Dictionary
(large print edition)
Young Readers' Thesaurus
(large print edition)

For further information or a free brochure, please contact us at:
Ulverscroft Large Print Books Ltd.,
The Green, Bradgate Road, Anstey,
Leicester, LE7 7FU, England.
Tel: (00 44) 0116 236 4325
Fax: (00 44) 0116 234 0205

CHISHOLM TRAIL SHOWDOWN

Jack Tregarth

For the young men in the Texas town of Indian Falls, riding the Chisholm Trail as cowboys is a rite of passage. Dan Lewis is heartbroken when it looks as though he is to be cheated of his chance. Determinedly, he manages to secure a place on the trail, but his joy quickly fades as he is accused of cattle rustling and nearly lynched. As he fights to clear his name, he finds himself up against a gang of the most ruthless men in the state . . .